Dugan yanked the wheel to the left to avoid crashing into the other vehicle, then swung the SUV to the side of the road and threw it in Park.

He jumped out and ran toward the burning vehicle.

The driver had shot at them. Tried to kill them.

Why? Because she was asking questions about her son?

She jerked herself from her immobilized state and climbed out. Dugan circled the car, peering into the window as if looking for a way to get the driver out. But the gas tank blew, another explosion sounded and flames engulfed the vehicle.

Sweat beaded on her forehead, the heat scalding her. She backed away, hugging the side of the SUV as she watched Dugan. He must have realized it was impossible to save the driver because he strode back toward her, his expression grim.

"Someone doesn't like us asking questions, Sage. But that means we might be on the right track to finding some answers."

COLD CASE AT COBRA CREEK

RITA HERRON

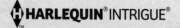
HARLEQUIN® INTRIGUE®

To all the Harlequin Intrigue fans—thanks for reading me
all these years!

Recycling programs
for this product may
not exist in your area.

ISBN-13: 978-0-373-69798-4

Cold Case at Cobra Creek

Copyright © 2014 by Rita B. Herron

Printed in U.S.A.

www.Harlequin.com

ABOUT THE AUTHOR

Award-winning author Rita Herron wrote her first book when she was twelve, but didn't think real people grew up to be writers. Now she writes so she doesn't have to get a *real* job. A former kindergarten teacher and workshop leader, she traded storytelling to kids for writing romance, and now she writes romantic comedies and romantic suspense. She lives in Georgia with her own romance hero and three kids. She loves to hear from readers, so please write her at P.O. Box 921225, Norcross, GA 30092-1225, or visit her website, www.ritaherron.com.

Books by Rita Herron

HARLEQUIN INTRIGUE

CAST OF CHARACTERS

Sage Freeport—Her son, Benji, has been missing for two years—is he dead or alive?

Dugan Graystone—This expert tracker will do anything to find Benji and bring him home for Christmas.

Sheriff Gandt—He thinks he owns the town—how far will he go to keep it that way?

Ron Lewis—Sage's fiancé ran off with Benji and ended up dead. Did the man's killer take Sage's son?

Donnell Ernest—Ron conned him out of his land—did he murder Ron Lewis?

Wilbur Rankins—He killed himself out of shame over letting Lewis rob him of his land—but was his death really a suicide?

Lloyd Riley—Did he kill Lewis to regain control of his ranch?

Janelle Dougasville—Lewis's foster sister. Does she know what he did with Benji?

Eloise Bremmer, Maude Handleman and Carol Tinsley—Lewis's former girlfriends and/or wives. Did one of them kill him when they discovered he'd lied to them?

Sandra Peyton—Lewis's first love. Does she know where Benji is?

Prologue

Sage Freeport vowed never to trust a man again.

Not after the way Trace Lanier had treated her. Promises of love and happily ever after—until she'd gotten pregnant.

Then those promises had evaporated, like rain on a strip of scorching-hot pavement.

Her three-year-old Benji had never met his father. She'd worried about him not having a man in his life and done her best to be two parents in one. Still, she couldn't throw a softball worth a darn, and baiting her own hook to go fishing at the pond literally made her feel faint.

Then Ron Lewis had come along a few months ago and swept her off her feet with his kindness and intelligence—and treated Benji like his own son.

Her gaze strayed to the tabletop tree she and Benji had decorated just yesterday. Together they'd made ornaments to hang on the tree, and when he was asleep last night, she'd wrapped his gift. He was going to be ecstatic on Christmas morning to find the softball and glove he'd asked for.

She pulled a pan of homemade cinnamon rolls from the oven to let them cool before her guests at the B and B she owned surfaced for breakfast, then went upstairs to check on her son.

Benji was normally up by now, underfoot in the kitchen when she was cooking—chatting and asking questions and sneaking bacon as soon as she took it off the pan.

But when she opened Benji's door, he wasn't in bed. A few toys were scattered around the floor, a sign he'd gotten up to play after she'd tucked him in the night before.

Figuring he was playing some imaginary game, she darted into his bathroom.

But he wasn't there, either.

She checked under his bed and frowned. "Benji? Where are you, honey?"

No answer.

Her heartbeat stuttered for a moment, but she told herself not to panic. The inn was a big house. The B and B held eight rooms, although most of them were empty at the time. With the holidays approaching, most people were staying home, going to visit family or flying to some exotic location for a winter vacation, not visiting small-town Texas.

She peeked inside Benji's closet but didn't see him. Yet the dresser drawer stood open, and his clothes looked as if he'd pawed through them.

Probably to dress himself. He was three and starting to vie for independence that way. She just had to teach him how to match colors now.

Then she noticed his backpack was missing.

Her heart suddenly racing, she turned and looked at his room again. The big bear he normally slept with wasn't in his bed. Not on the floor or in the room at all. Neither was the whistle he liked or his favorite red hat.

But his blanket was there. He'd never go anywhere without that blue blanket.

Fear seized her, but she fought it off.

Surely Benji was just pretending he was on a camping trip. He and Ron had been talking about hiking the other night. Ron had even asked Benji which one of his special friends/toys he would carry with him if he was going on a long trip.

The bear, whistle and red cap were on his list.

Her hands shaking as other scenarios taunted her, she raced down the hall to the empty rooms and searched inside. No Benji.

Hating to disturb the two guests she did have but panicked now, she knocked on the door to the Ellises', an elderly couple on an anniversary trip. The gray-haired man opened the door dressed in a robe. "Yeah?"

"I'm sorry, Mr. Ellis, but have you seen my son, Benji?"

"No, ma'am. Me and Henrietta been sleeping."

"Would you mind checking your room in case he snuck in? He's only three and mischievous at times."

He scratched his head, sending his wiry hair askew. "Sure." He left the door open, and Sage watched as he checked under the bed, the closet and adjoining bathroom. "Sorry, Ms. Freeport, he's not in here."

Sage's stomach knotted. If—no, *when*—she found Benji, she would explain that hiding from her was not okay.

She climbed the steps to the third-floor attic room. A woman named Elvira had chosen it, saying she needed solace and to be alone. The poor woman had lost a child, and Sage had given her privacy to mourn.

But Elvira didn't answer. Sage let herself in and found a note from the lady saying she'd decided to leave early and didn't want to disturb Sage.

Benji liked this room because the window offered a view of the creek behind the house.

But the room was empty.

Nerves on edge, she ran downstairs, once again checking each room and shouting Benji's name. She rushed outside, wind beating at her as she searched the yard, the garden out back, the swing set, the fort and the tree house.

Benji was nowhere to be found.

Terrified, she ran back inside to call the sheriff. But the phone was ringing as she entered the kitchen. Maybe a neighbor had found Benji.

She grabbed the phone, determined to get rid of the caller so she could phone the sheriff. But his voice echoed back.

"Ms. Freeport, it's Sheriff Gandt."

Her stomach pitched. "Yes, I was just about to call you. My little boy, Benji… He's gone."

"I was afraid of that," Sheriff Gandt muttered.

Icy fear seized Sage.

"I think you'd better come down to River Road Crossing at Cobra Creek."

"Why?" She had to swallow to make her voice work. "Is Benji there?"

"Just meet me there."

He hung up, and Sage's knees buckled. She grabbed the kitchen counter to keep from hitting the floor.

No…Benji was fine. He had to be…

She grabbed her keys and ran outside. The minivan took three tries to crank, but she threw it in gear and tore down the road toward the river crossing.

As soon as she rounded the bend, she spotted flames shooting into the air. Smoke curled upward, clogging the sky in a thick, gray blanket.

Tires squealed as she swung the van to the shoulder of the road, jumped out and ran toward the burning car.

Sheriff Gandt stood by while firemen worked to extinguish the blaze. But even with the flames and smoke, she could tell that the car was a black Jeep.

Ron drove a black Jeep.

"Do you recognize this vehicle?" the sheriff asked.

A cold sweat broke out on Sage's body. "It's Ron's. My fiancé."

Sheriff Gandt's expression looked harsh in the morning light. Then she saw what he was holding in his hands.

Benji's teddy bear and red hat.

No… Dear God. Had Benji been in the car with Ron when it crashed and caught on fire?

Chapter One

Two years later

Dugan Graystone did not trust Sheriff Billy Gandt worth a damn.

Gandt thought he owned the town and the people in it and made no bones about the fact that men like Dugan, men who weren't white, weren't fit for office and should stay out of his way.

Gandt had even tried to stop Dugan from taking on this search-and-rescue mission, saying he could use his own men. But the families of the two lost hikers had heard about Dugan's reputation as an expert tracker and insisted he spearhead the efforts to find the young men.

Dugan rode his stallion across the wilderness, scrutinizing every bush and tree, along with the soil, for footprints and other signs that someone had come this way. A team of searchers had spread across the miles of forests looking for the missing men, but Dugan had a sixth sense, and it had led him over to Cobra Creek, miles from where Gandt had set up base camp for the volunteer workers involved in the search.

Dammit, he hated Gandt. He'd run against him for sheriff and lost—mainly because Gandt bought votes. But one day he'd put the bastard in his place and prove that beneath that good-old-boy act, Gandt was nothing but a lying, cheating coward.

Born on the reservation near Cobra Creek, Dugan had Native American blood running through his veins. Dugan fought for what was right.

And nothing about Gandt was right.

Money, power and women were Gandt's for the taking. And crime—if it benefited Billy—could be overlooked for a price.

Though Dugan owned his own spread, on the side, he worked as a P.I. His friend, Texas Ranger Jaxon Ward, was looking into Gandt's financials, determined to catch the man at his own game.

The recent flooding of the creek had uprooted bushes and trees, and washed up debris from the river that connected to the creek. Dugan noted an area that looked trampled, as if a path had been cut through the woods.

He guided his horse to a tree and dismounted, then knelt to examine the still-damp earth. A footprint in the mud?

Was it recent?

He noticed another, then some brush flattened, leading toward the creek. Dugan's instincts kicked in, and he shone his flashlight on the ground and followed the indentations.

Several feet away, he saw another area of ground that looked disturbed. Mud and sticks and…something else.

Bones.

Maybe an animal's?

He hurried over to examine them, his pulse pounding. No…that was a human femur. And a finger.

Human bones.

And judging from the decomp, they had been there too long to belong to one of the two teenagers who'd gone missing.

The radio at his belt buzzed and crackled, and he hit the button to connect.

"We found the boys," Jaxon said. "A little dehydrated, but they're fine."

Dugan removed his Stetson and wiped sweat from his forehead. "Good. But I need the coroner over here at Cobra Creek."

"What?"

"I found bones," Dugan said. "Looks like they've been here a couple of years."

A foreboding washed over Dugan. Two years ago, a man named Ron Lewis had supposedly died in a car crash near here. Sage Freeport's son had been with him at the time.

The man's body and her son's had never been found.

Could these bones belong to Ron Lewis, the man who'd taken her son?

SAGE SET A PLACE at the breakfast bar for Benji, then slid a pancake onto the plate and doused it with powdered sugar, just the way her son liked it. His chocolate milk came next.

The tabletop Christmas tree she kept year-round still held the tiny ornaments Benji had made and hung on it. And the present she'd had for him the year he'd gone missing still sat wrapped, waiting for his small hands to tear it open.

It was a glove and ball, something Benji had asked Santa for that year.

Would the glove still fit when she finally found him and he came home?

Two of her guests, a couple named Dannon, who'd come to Cobra Creek to celebrate their twentieth anniversary, gave her pitying looks, but she ignored them.

She knew people thought she was crazy. Mrs. Kran-dall, the owner of the diner in town, had even warned her that perpetuating the fantasy that her son was still alive by keeping a place set for him was dangerous for her and downright creepy.

She also suggested that it would hurt Sage's business.

A business Sage needed to pay the bills—and to keep her sanity.

But she couldn't accept that her son was dead.

Not without answers as to why Ron had taken Benji from the house and where they'd been headed.

Not without definite proof that he wasn't alive out there somewhere, needing her.

Of course, Benji's hat and bear had been found at the scene, but his bones had never been recovered.

Sheriff Gandt theorized that Lewis and Benji probably had been injured and tried to escape the fire by going into the creek. But storms created a strong current that night, and their bodies must have washed downstream, then into the river where they'd never be found.

She should never have trusted Ron with her son. It was her fault he was gone....

She refused to believe that he wouldn't be back. She had to cling to hope.

Without it, the guilt would eat her alive.

DUGAN GRITTED HIS TEETH as Sheriff Gandt studied the bones.

"Could have been a stranger wandering through," Gandt said. "Miles of wilderness out here. I'll check the databases for wanted men. Criminals have been known to hide out here off the grid."

The medical examiner, Dr. Liam Longmire, narrowed his eyes as he examined the body they unearthed when they'd swept the debris from the bones. Most of the skeleton was intact. Of course, the bones had decayed and been mauled by animals, but there were enough that they'd be able to identify him. That is, if they had medical records to compare to.

"What about Ron Lewis?" Dugan asked. "It could be him."

Sheriff Gandt adjusted the waistband of his uniform pants and chewed on a blade of grass, his silence surprising. The man usually had an answer for everything.

Dr. Longmire looked up at Dugan, then Gandt. "I can't say who he is yet, but this man didn't die from a fire or from the elements."

"What was the cause of death?" Dugan asked.

Longmire pointed to the rib cage and thoracic cavity. "See the markings of a bullet? It shattered one of his ribs. I can tell more when I get him on the table, but judging from the angle, it appears the bullet probably pierced his heart."

Dugan glanced at Gandt, who made a harrumph sound.

"Guess you've got a murder to investigate, Sheriff," Dugan said.

Gandt met his gaze with stone-cold, gray eyes, then glanced at the M.E. "How long has he been dead?"

"My guess is a couple of years." Dr. Longmire paused. "That'd be about the time that Lewis man ran off with Sage Freeport's kid."

Gandt nodded, his mouth still working that blade of grass. But his grim expression told Dugan this body was more of a nuisance than a case he wanted to work.

"I'll request Lewis's dental records," Dr. Longmire said. "If they match, we'll know who our victim is."

Gandt started to walk away, but Dugan cleared his throat. "Sheriff, aren't you going to get a crime unit to comb the area and look for evidence?"

"Don't see no reason for that," Gandt muttered. "If the man's been dead two years, probably ain't nothin' to find. Besides, the flood last week would have washed away any evidence." He gestured to the south. "That said, Lewis's car was found farther downstream. If his body got in the water, it would have floated further downstream, not up here."

"Not if his body was dumped in a different place from where he died."

"You're grasping at straws." Gandt directed his comment to the M.E. "ID him and then we'll go from there."

The sheriff could be right. The victim could have been a drifter. Or a man from another town. Hell, he could have been one of the two prisoners who'd escaped jail a couple years back, ones who'd never been caught.

But the sheriff should at least be looking for evidence near where the body was found.

Gandt strode toward his squad car, and Dugan used his phone to take photographs of the bones. Dr. Longmire offered a commentary on other injuries he noted the body had sustained, and Dugan made a note of them.

Then Longmire directed the medics to load the body into the van to transport to the morgue, making sure they were careful to keep the skeleton intact and preserve any forensic evidence on the bones.

Dugan combed the area, scrutinizing the grass and embankment near where the bones had washed up. He also searched the brush for clues. He plucked a small scrap of fabric from a briar and found a metal button in the mud a few feet from the place where he'd first discovered the bones. He bagged the items for the lab to analyze, then conducted another sweep of the property, spanning out a half mile in both directions.

Unfortunately, Gandt was right. With time, weather and the animals foraging in the wilderness, he couldn't pinpoint if the body had gone into the river here or some other point.

Frustrated, he finally packed up and headed back to town.

But a bad feeling tightened his gut. Gandt had closed the case involving Sage Freeport's missing son and Lewis too quickly for his taste.

How would he handle this one?

By LATE AFTERNOON, news of the bones found at Cobra Creek reached Sage through the grapevine in the small Texas town. She was gathering groceries to bake her famous coconut cream pie when she overheard two women talking about the hikers that had been recovered safely.

The checkout lady, Lorraine Hersher, the cousin of the M.E., broke in. "A body was found out at the creek. Nothing but the bones left."

Sage inched her way up near the register.

"Who was it?" one of the women asked.

"Don't think they know yet. Liam said he was checking dental records. But he said the man had been dead about two years."

Sage's stomach clenched. Two years? About the time Ron's car had crashed.

Could it possibly be…?

Desperate for answers, she pushed her cart to the side, leaving her groceries inside it, then hurried toward the door. The sheriff's office was across the square, and she tugged her jacket around her, battling a stiff breeze as she crossed the street.

Sheriff Gandt had been less than helpful when Benji had gone missing. He wouldn't want her bugging him now.

But she'd long ago decided she didn't care what he thought.

She charged inside the office, surprised to see Dugan Graystone standing inside at the front desk. She'd seen the big man in town a few times, but he kept to himself. With his intense, dark brown eyes and brooding manner, some said he was a loner but that he was the best tracker in Texas. Tall, broad shoulders, sharp cheekbones—the package was handsome. Half the women in town thought he was sexy, while the other half were afraid of him.

Dr. Longmire stood next to him, the sheriff on the opposite side of the desk.

All three men turned to look at her as she entered, looking like they'd been caught doing something wrong.

Sage lifted her chin in a show of bravado. "I heard about the body you found at Cobra Creek."

Dugan's brown eyes met hers, turmoil darkening the depths, while Gandt shot her one of his condescending looks. She couldn't believe the man had ever been married and understood why he wasn't anymore.

She had heard that he'd taken in his ailing mother, that the elderly woman was wheelchair-bound, difficult and demanding. Even though she disliked Gandt, she had to admit his loyalty to his mother was admirable.

"Who was it?" Sage asked.

Dr. Longmire adjusted his hat, acknowledging her with a politeness bred from a different era. "The body belonged to Ron Lewis."

Sage gasped. "You're sure?"

"Dental and medical records confirm it," the M.E. said.

Sage's legs threatened to give way. She caught herself by dropping onto a chair across from the desk. Tears clogged her throat as panic and fear seized her.

But she'd been in the dark for two years, and she had to know the truth.

Even if it killed her.

"Was Benji with him?"

Chapter Two

Sage held her breath. "Sheriff, did you find Benji?"

Sheriff Gandt shook his head. "No. Just Lewis's body."

Relief spilled through Sage. "Then my son... He may still be out there. He may be alive."

Dugan and the medical examiner traded questioning looks, but the sheriff's frown made her flinch. Did he know something he wasn't telling her? Was that the reason he'd closed the case so quickly after Benji disappeared?

"Ms. Freeport," Sheriff Gandt said in a tone he might use with a child, "Dr. Longmire believes Ron Lewis has been dead since the day of that crash. That means that your son has been, too. We just haven't found his body yet. Probably because of the elements—"

"That's enough, Sheriff," Dugan said sharply.

Sheriff Gandt shot Dugan an irritated look. "I believe your part is done here, Graystone."

Sage gripped the edge of the desk. "How did Ron die, Sheriff?"

"Ms. Freeport, why don't you go home and calm down—"

"He died of a gunshot wound," Dugan said, cutting off the sheriff.

Sage barely stifled a gasp. "Then the car crash...? That didn't kill him."

"No," Dr. Longmire said, "he most likely bled out."

Sage's mind raced. Who had shot Ron? And why? "The shot caused the crash," she said, piecing together a scenario in her head.

"That would be my guess," Dr. Longmire said.

"Was there a bullet hole in the car?" Dugan asked Gandt.

Sheriff Gandt shrugged. "I don't know. The fire destroyed most of it."

Sage folded her arms and stared at the sheriff. "But that bullet proves Ron Lewis's death was no accident. He was murdered."

DUGAN WORKED TO rein in his anger toward Gandt. The weasel should be comforting Sage and reassuring her he'd do everything humanly possible to find the truth about what happened to her son.

That was what he'd do if he was sheriff.

But he lacked the power and money the Gandts had, and in this small town, that seemed to mean everything.

"It appears that way," Sheriff Gandt told Sage. "And I will be investigating the matter. But—" he lifted a warning hand to Sage "—if your son had survived, we would have found him by now, Ms. Freeport. Odds are that the shooter fired at Lewis, he crashed and managed to get out of the car and fled. Maybe your son was with him, maybe not. But if he made it to the water with Lewis, he couldn't have survived the frigid temperature or the current. He would have been swept downstream and drowned."

"Sheriff," Dugan snarled, hating the man's cold bluntness.

The M.E. gave Sage a sympathetic look, then excused himself and hurried out the door.

Sheriff Gandt tugged at his pants. Damn man needed a belt to keep the things up. That or lose thirty pounds around his belly so he didn't have to wear them so low.

"I know you want me to sugarcoat things, Graystone, but I'm the sheriff, not a damn counselor. I tell it like it is. Good or bad."

Still, he could consider Sage's feelings. She'd lost a child. "Part of your job is to protect innocent citizens and to find out the truth when something happens to one of them. Benji Freeport was three. He was certainly innocent." Dugan squared off with the sheriff. "But you haven't done a damn thing to give his mother closure or find the answers she needs."

"You think bringing her a mangled bunch of bones is going to make her feel better?" Sheriff Gandt said.

"That would hurt, but at least I'd know the truth," Sage said. "And now that we know Ron was murdered, there is a chance that whoever shot him took Benji." Sage's voice cracked. "That means that Benji may be out there, alone, in trouble, needing me. That he's been waiting for us to find him all this time."

Dugan's chest tightened at the emotions in her voice. Emotions she had every right to feel, because she'd spoken the truth.

Sheriff Gandt swung a crooked finger toward the door. "I don't need either of you telling me how to do my job. Now, leave so I can get to it."

"Then let me know what you find." Sage clutched her shoulder bag, turned and walked out the door.

Dugan stared at the sheriff. "She deserves to know what happened to her son. And if he's alive, she deserves to bring him home."

"She's deluding herself if she thinks she'll find him alive," Sheriff Gandt said. "She needs to accept that he's gone and move on with her life."

Dugan had never had a child, but if he did and that child disappeared, he'd move heaven and earth to find him. "You are going to investigate Lewis's murder, aren't you? After all, you owe it to the people in the town to make sure that his killer isn't still among them."

Gandt tapped his badge. "In case you've forgotten, Graystone, the people elected me, so they obviously have confidence in my abilities. Now, get out of my office."

Dugan shot him a go-to-hell look, turned and stormed out the door. The man might make a token gesture to solve Lewis's murder.

But he doubted he would put forth any effort to hunt for Benji Freeport.

Dugan spotted Sage sitting on a park bench in the square, her face buried in her hands, her body trembling.

He headed across the square to join her. If Gandt wouldn't find Sage's son for her, he would.

SAGE WAS SO ANGRY she was shaking all over. Sheriff Gandt had stonewalled her before.

But how could he dismiss her so easily now that they knew that Ron Lewis had been murdered?

Ron's face flashed in her mind, and her stomach revolted. She'd been such a fool to trust him. Why had he taken her son with him that day? Where was he going?

And who had killed him?

The questions ate at her. None of it made sense.

Ron had waltzed into her life and charmed her with his good looks, his business sense and his talk of giving the town a face-lift and bringing in tourism. Tourists would have greatly impacted her income, so she'd been on board from the beginning.

Maybe that was the one reason he'd warmed up to her. Had he thought she could influence the town council with his plans for putting Cobra Creek on the map?

Footsteps crunched on gravel, and she suddenly felt someone beside her. A hand on her shoulder.

She jerked her head up, wiping at the tears streaming

down her face, and stared into Dugan Graystone's dark eyes. The man was a rebel of sorts and was the only person she'd ever known to go up against the sheriff.

High cheekbones sculpted an angular face, evidence of his Native American roots. His chiseled face was bronzed from work on the ranch, his hands were broad and strong looking, his big body made for ranching and working the land.

Or for a woman.

She silently chided herself. Just because she felt vulnerable and needy, and Dugan was strong and powerful looking, didn't mean she'd fall prey to his charms.

No man would ever get close to her again.

"What do you want?" Sage asked, a little more harshly than she'd intended.

Dugan's eyes flared at her tone. "Gandt is a first-class jerk."

His comment deflated her anger, and a nervous laugh escaped her. "Yes, he is."

"He said he'd look into Lewis's murder."

"Sure he will." Sage brushed her hands together. "Like he looked into the crash two years ago."

Dugan sank his big body onto the bench beside her. "I know you were engaged to Lewis and want answers about who killed him."

Anger shot through Sage. "We may have been engaged, but that was obviously a mistake. The minute he took my son from my house without my permission, any feelings I had for him died." She swallowed the lump in her throat. "I don't care why he was murdered. In fact, I would have killed him myself for taking Benji if I'd found him."

A tense second passed. "I understand," Dugan said in a gruff voice.

"Do you? That man took everything from me."

The anguish in her tone made his chest squeeze. "I'll help you," he said. "I'll find out why Lewis was murdered."

Sage studied his face. He seemed so sincere. Earnest. As if he actually cared.

But she wouldn't buy in to that, not ever again.

On the other hand, Dugan had run for sheriff and Gandt had beaten him, so he probably had his own personal agenda. He wanted to show Gandt up and prove to the town that they'd elected the wrong man.

She really didn't care about his motive. "All right. But understand this—the only reason I want to know who killed Ron is that it might lead me to my son. Whatever dirt you dig up on Ron is fine with me. I don't care about his reputation or even my own, for that matter."

Dugan studied her in silence for a few minutes. Sage felt the wind ruffle her hair, felt the heat from his body, felt the silence thick with the unknown.

"I'll do everything I can to help you," Dugan said gruffly. "But I may not find the answers you want."

Sage understood the implications of his statement. "I know that." She gripped her hands together. "All I want is the truth…no matter what it is."

"Even if it's not pretty?"

Sage nodded. "The truth can't be any worse than what I've already imagined."

DUGAN HOPED THAT was true. But there was the possibility that they'd find out her little boy had been burned in the fire. Or that he'd been kidnapped by a cold-blooded murderer.

The scenarios that came to mind sent a shot of fear through him. For all they knew, the shooter could have abducted Benji and sold him or handed him off to a group trafficking kids. Hell, he could have been a pedophile.

In fact, kidnapping the boy could have been the end-game all along.

Someone could have hired Lewis to get the boy.

But if so, why?

He had to ask questions, questions Sage might not like.

"You've done investigative work before?" Sage asked.

Dugan nodded. "I've been called in as a consultant on some cold cases. I have a friend, Texas Ranger Jaxon Ward, who I work with."

"How do you know him?"

"We go way back," Dugan said, remembering the foster home where they'd met.

Sage arched an eyebrow in question, but Dugan let the moment pass. They weren't here to talk about him and his shady upbringing. "In light of the fact that Lewis's body has been found, I'm going to enter your son's picture into the system for missing children."

Emotions darkened Sage's soft green eyes, but she nodded. "Of course. I tried to get Sheriff Gandt to do that two years ago, but he was certain Benji died in the crash or drowned, and said it was a waste of time."

That sounded like shoddy police work to him.

"If you want to stop by the inn, I can give you one of the latest pictures I took."

"I'll walk with you over there now."

Sage stood, one hand clutching her shoulder bag. "Why don't you meet me there in half an hour? I have an errand to run first."

"Half an hour," Dugan agreed.

Sage hesitated a moment, her breath shaky in the heart-beat of silence that stretched between them. "Thank you, Dugan. I can't tell you what it means to have someone listen to me. I...know some people think I'm nuts. That I just can't let go."

He had heard rumors that she set the table for her son at every meal, as if he was coming home for dinner. Hell, was that crazy, or was she simply trying to keep hope alive?

"I don't blame you for not giving up," Dugan said gruffly. "At least not without the facts or proof that your son is really gone."

He let the words linger between them, well aware she understood the meaning underscoring his comment. If he found proof Benji was dead, she'd have to accept that.

But if there was a chance the boy was out there somewhere, he'd find him and bring him back to her where he belonged.

SAGE UNLOADED THE GROCERIES, grateful the couple staying at the inn had taken a day trip and wouldn't be back until bedtime. Breakfast came with the room rental, but lunch and dinner were optional. In addition, she provided coffee and tea and snacks midmorning and afternoon, including fruit, cookies and an assortment of freshly baked pastries and desserts. She usually conferred with the guests on check-in and planned accordingly.

The doorbell rang; then the front bell tinkled that someone had entered. She rushed to the entryway and found Dugan standing beneath the chandelier, studying the rustic farm tools and pictures of horses on the wall.

People who visited Texas wanted rustic charm, and she tried to give it to them.

"I came for that picture." Dugan tipped his Stetson out of politeness, his rugged features stark in the evening light.

"Come this way." She led him through the swinging double doors to the kitchen. His gaze caught on the tabletop Christmas tree, and she bit back a comment, refusing to explain herself.

Maybe Benji would never come back.

But if he did, his present would be waiting. And they would celebrate all the days and holidays they'd missed spending together the past two years.

Chapter Three

Sage opened a photo album on the breakfast bar and began to flip through it. Dugan watched pain etch itself on her face as she stared at the pictures chronicling Benji's young life.

A baby picture of him swaddled in a blue blanket while he lay nestled in Sage's arms. A photo of the little boy sleeping in a crib, another of him as an infant in the bathtub playing with a rubber ducky, pictures of him learning to crawl, then walk.

Photos of Benji tearing open presents at his first birthday party, riding a rocking horse at Christmas, playing in the sprinkler out back, cuddled on the couch in monster pajamas and cradling his blanket.

Sage paused to trace her finger over a small envelope. "I kept a lock of Benji's hair from his first haircut."

Dugan offered a smile, tolerating her trip down memory lane because he understood her emotions played into this case and he couldn't ignore them.

He shifted uncomfortably. He had a hard time relating to family; he had never been part of one and didn't know how families worked. At least, not normal, loving ones. If they existed.

He'd grown up between foster care and the rez, never really wanted in either place.

She brushed at a tear, then removed a picture of Benji posed by the Christmas tree. "I took that the day before he went missing."

Dugan glanced at the tabletop tree and realized the same present still lay beneath the tree's base. Dammit. She'd kept the tree up all this time waiting on her son to return to open it.

"Can I get the photograph back?" Sage asked. "As you can see, this is all I have left...."

The crack in her voice tore at him. "Of course. I'll take good care of it, Sage." And maybe he'd bring back the real thing instead of just a picture.

But he refrained from making that promise.

"Sage, before I get started, we need to talk. There are some questions I need you to answer."

Sage closed the photo album and laid a hand on top of it. He noticed her nails were short, slightly jagged, as if she'd been biting them.

"What do you want to know?"

"Do you have any idea why Ron Lewis had Benji in the car with him that day?"

"No." Sage threaded her fingers through the long, tangled tresses of her hair, hair that was streaked with red, brown and gold. "Sheriff Gandt suggested that he was taking Benji Christmas shopping to buy me a present."

A possibility. "What do you think?"

"Ron knew how protective I was of my son. I don't understand why he would have left without telling me or leaving me a note. He knew that Benji was all I had, and that I would panic when I woke up and discovered they were gone."

"What about other family?" Dugan asked.

Sage sighed wearily. "I never knew my father. My mother died the year before I had Benji. A car accident."

He knew this could get touchy. "And Benji's father?"

Resignation settled in her eyes. "Trace Lanier. I met him right after my mother died." She traced a finger along the edge of the photo album. "I was grieving and vulnerable. Not that that's an excuse, but we dated a few times. When I discovered the pregnancy, he bailed."

"Where is he now?"

"I have no clue. He worked the rodeos, traveling town to town."

"Did he express any interest in seeing his son?"

Sage laughed, a bitter sound. "No. He didn't even want to acknowledge that Benji was his. In fact, he accused me of lying, of coming after him for money."

Dugan waited, his pulse hammering. Sage didn't strike him as that type at all.

"I was furious," Sage said. "I told him that my mother was a single mother and that she'd raised me on her own, and that I would do the same. I didn't want his money. And I didn't care if I ever saw him again or if he ever met his son."

"And that was that?"

Sage brushed her hands together. "That was that. I never heard from him again."

Dugan contemplated her story. "Do you think that he might have changed his mind and decided he wanted to see Benji?"

Sage shook her head. "No. I think he's doing pretty well in the rodeo circuit now. Making a name bronco riding. That brings the rodeo groupies. The last thing he'd want is to have a child get in the way of that."

Dugan had never met the bastard, but he didn't like him.

Still, he'd verify that information. Perhaps Lanier's manager had suggested that having a little boy could improve his popularity. It was a long shot, but Dugan didn't intend to ignore any possibility.

SAGE HATED ADMITTING that she had fallen for Trace Lanier's sexy rodeo looks, but she had. Even worse, she'd believed Ron Lewis was different.

Could he have simply been taking Benji Christmas shopping and gotten killed before he could bring her son back?

And why would someone kill Ron?

Or had Ron taken Benji for another reason?

But why? She didn't have money to pay a ransom....

"Do you want coffee?" Sage asked.

Dugan nodded, and she poured them both a mug, then placed a slice of homemade pound cake on a plate in front of him. "It's fresh. I baked it last night."

A small smile curved his mouth. "I've heard you're a good cook."

"Really?" Sage blushed. What else had he heard?

"Yes, I'm sure it helps with your business."

"I suppose so," Sage said. "I used to stay with my grandma when I was little, and she taught me everything she knew."

He sipped his coffee. "Tell me about Ron Lewis. How did you two meet?"

"Actually he stayed here when he came to town on business," Sage said. "He was a real estate developer. He wanted to convince the town council to go forward on a new development that would enrich the town, create jobs and tourism and bring us out of the Dark Ages."

"I remember hearing something about that project," Dugan said, although he hadn't exactly been for the development. The group handling it wanted to buy up ranches and farms in the neighboring area, and turn Cobra Creek into a tourist trap with outlet malls, fast-food chains and a dude ranch.

"So you struck up a friendship?"

Sage nodded. "I was reluctant at first, but he was persistent. And he took an interest in Benji."

"Benji liked him?"

"Yes."

"He would have gone with him, without being afraid?"

"Yes," Sage said, her voice cracking. "Ron stayed in Cobra Creek most of that summer, so we went on several family outings together." She'd thought she'd finally found a man who loved her and her son.

Fool.

Dugan broke off a chunk of cake and put it in his mouth. Sage watched a smile flicker in his eyes, one that pleased her more than it should.

"Did the town council approve his plans?"

Sage gave a noncommittal shrug. "They were going back and forth on things, discussing it." She frowned at Dugan. "Do you think his murder had something to do with the development?"

"I don't know," Dugan said. "But it's worth looking into."

Sage contemplated his suggestion. She should have asked more questions about Ron's business, about the investors he said he had lined up, about *him*.

And now it was too late. If something had gone wrong with his business, something that had gotten him killed, he might have taken that secret with him to the grave.

DUGAN NEEDED TO ask around, find out more about how the locals felt about Lewis's proposal. What had happened to the development after his death? Had anyone profited?

But Sage's comment about Ron's interest in Benji made him pause. "You said he showed an interest in Benji?"

Sage stirred sweetener in her coffee. "Yes, some men

don't like kids. Others don't know how to talk to them, but Ron seemed…comfortable with Benji."

"Hmm," Dugan mumbled. "Did he come from a big family?"

Sage frowned. "No, I asked him that. And he actually looked kind of sad. He said he was an only child and lost his parents when he was young."

"Was he married before? Maybe he had a child."

"No, at least he said he'd never married," Sage said. "But at this point, I don't know what to believe. Everything he told me could have been a lie."

True. In fact, he could have planned to kidnap Benji all along. He'd warmed up to the boy so he'd go with him willingly.

But why?

For money? Maybe someone had paid him to take Benji, then killed Ron Lewis to get rid of any witnesses.

But why would anyone want to kidnap Benji?

Sage wasn't wealthy, and she had no family that could offer a big reward. Kidnappers had been known to abduct a child to force a parent into doing something for them, but if swaying the town council to vote for the development had been the issue, it wouldn't have worked. Sage had no power or influence in the town.

Then again, Dugan had no proof that Ron Lewis had done anything wrong. That the man hadn't been sincerely in love with Sage, that he hadn't come to the town to help it prosper, that he was an innocent who had been shot to death for some reason.

And that he might have died trying to save Sage's son.

"Did Lewis leave anything of his here at the inn? A calendar? Computer?"

"No, I don't think so," Sage said.

"I know it's been two years, but what room did he stay in?"

"The Cross-ties Room."

He arched an eyebrow.

"I named each room based on a theme. People who come to Cobra Creek want the atmosphere, the feel of the quaint western town."

"Can I see that room, or is someone staying in it?"

"You can see it," Sage said. "I have only one couple staying here now. They're in the Water Tower Room."

Sage led Dugan up the stairs to the second floor. She unlocked the room, then stood back and watched as he studied the room.

"Have you rented this room since he was here?"

"Yes, a couple of times," she said. "I was full capacity during the art festival both years."

He walked over and looked inside the dresser, checking each drawer, but they were empty. Next he searched the drawers in the oak desk in the corner. Again, nothing.

"What are you looking for?" Sage asked.

Dugan shrugged. "If Lewis was killed because he was into something illegal, there might be evidence he left behind." He opened the closet door and looked inside. "Did he take everything with him that day when he left?"

Sage nodded. "His suitcase and computer were gone. That was what freaked me out."

"If he'd simply been taking Benji shopping, he wouldn't have taken those things with him."

"Exactly." Sage's heart stuttered as she remembered the blind panic that had assaulted her.

"Did he mention that he was leaving town to you?" Dugan asked.

"The day before, he said he might have to go away for a business meeting, but that he'd be back before Christmas."

"Did he say where the meeting was?"

Sage pushed a strand of hair away from her face. "No… but then, I didn't bother to ask." Guilt hit her again. "I was so distracted, so caught up in the holidays, in making a stupid grocery list for Christmas dinner and finishing my shopping, that I didn't pay much attention." Her voice broke. "If I had, maybe I would have picked up on something."

Dugan's boots clicked on the floor as he strode over to the doorway, where she stood. "Sage, this is not your fault."

"Yes, it is," Sage said, her heart breaking all over again. "I was Benji's mother. I was supposed to protect him."

"You did everything you could."

"Then, why is he missing?" Sage asked. "Why isn't he here with me this year, wrapping presents and making sugar cookies?"

"I don't know," Dugan said in a low voice. "But I promise you that I'll find out."

Sage latched on to the hope Dugan offered. But the same terrifying images that haunted her at night flashed behind her eyes now.

If the person who'd shot Ron had abducted Benji, what had he done with him? Where was he? And what had happened to him over the past two years?

Was he taken care of or had he been abused? Was he hungry? Alone?

Would he remember her when they found him?

"THEY FOUND LEWIS'S BODY."

"Dammit. How did that happen?"

"Floods washed the body up. That Indian uncovered his bones in the bushes when he was looking for those hikers that got lost."

"After two years, they identified Lewis?"

"Yes. Damn dental records. I should have extracted all his teeth."

A tense second passed. "Hell, you should have burned the bastard's body in that car."

"I thought it was taken care of."

"Yeah, well, it wasn't. And Sage Freeport is asking questions again. Knowing her, she'll be pushing to get the case reopened. She's like a bloodhound."

"If she doesn't settle down, I'll take care of her."

"This time make sure nothing can come back to haunt us."

"No problem. When she disappears, it'll be for good."

Chapter Four

"Did Lewis always stay in this same room?" Dugan asked.

"Yes."

"How long was he here?"

Sage rubbed her temple. "The first time he came, he stayed a couple of weeks. Then he left for a month. When he returned, he stayed about six months."

"Where did he go when he left?"

"He was traveling around Texas. Said he worked with this company that looked for property across the state, small towns that were in need of rebuilding. Part of his job was to scout out the country and make suggestions to them."

"Where was his home?"

Sage straightened a pillow on top of the homemade quilt, which had imprints of horses on the squares. "He said he was from South Texas, I think. That he grew up in a little town not too far from Laredo."

Dugan made a mental note to check out his story. Maybe someone in that town knew more about Lewis.

He walked through the room again, the boards creaking beneath his boots as he stepped inside the closet. His toe caught on something and when he looked down, he realized a plank was loose.

He knelt and ran his finger along the wooden slat, his senses prickling. Was something beneath the board?

He yanked at it several times, and it finally gave way. He pulled it free, laid it to the side and felt the one next to it. It was loose, too, so he tugged it free, as well.

His curiosity spiking, he peered beneath the flooring. Something yellow caught his eye. He slid his hand below and felt inside the hole. His fingers connected with a small manila envelope.

"What are you doing?" Sage asked over his shoulder.

"Something's under here." He wiggled his fingers until he snagged the envelope, then removed it from the hole.

"What is that?" Sage asked.

"I don't know, but we'll find out." Dugan felt again just to make sure there wasn't anything else lodged beneath the floor, but the space was empty. Standing, he walked back to the corner desk, opened the envelope and dumped it upside down.

Sage gasped as the contents spilled out. "What in the world?"

Dugan picked up a driver's license and flipped it open. A picture of Ron Lewis stared back at him.

But the name on the license read Mike Martin.

"That's a fake driver's license," Sage said.

Dugan raked his hand over the lot of them, spreading a half dozen different licenses across the bed. "Each one of these has a different name."

"My God, Dugan," Sage whispered. "Ron Lewis wasn't his real name."

"No." Dugan met her gaze. Aliases indicated the man might have been a professional con man. "And if he lied about who he was, no telling what else he lied about."

SAGE SANK ONTO the bed, in shock. "I can't believe he lied to me, that he had all these other identities." She felt like such a fool. "Why would he do that, Dugan? Why come here and make me think he was someone else? Just to make me fall for him?"

Dugan's mouth flattened. "Do you have a lot of money, Sage?"

"No." She gestured around the room. "I put everything into remodeling this house as a bed and breakfast."

"You don't have a trust fund somewhere?"

"God, no," Sage said, embarrassed to admit the truth, "I'm in debt up to my eyeballs."

"Then he didn't fabricate his lies to swindle you out of money," Dugan said. "My guess is that this business of a land development was some kind of sham. You just happened to get caught in the middle."

"So, he never really cared for me," Sage said. She'd asked herself that a thousand times the past two years, but facing the truth was humiliating. It also meant she'd endangered her son by falling for Ron Lewis's lies.

Dugan's apologetic look made her feel even more like an idiot.

"Even if he was running a con, maybe he really did fall in love with you and Benji," Dugan suggested.

"Yeah," Sage said wryly. "Maybe he was going to change for me." She picked up one of the fake IDs, read the name, then threw it against the wall. "More like, he took me for a moron and used me." She studied another name, her mind racing. "But why take Benji that day?"

"I don't know." Dugan shrugged. "Did he know about your debt?"

Sage nodded. "He told me not to worry, that when this deal came through, my B and B would be overflowing with business and we'd make a fortune."

"Maybe he meant that," Dugan said. "Maybe he really wanted to make things better for you and your son."

Sage made a sound of disgust. "Like you said before,

Dugan, he lied about his name. What else was he lying about?" She scattered the IDs around, trying to recall if he'd mentioned any of the other names he'd used. "I can't believe I fell for everything he said." Because she'd been lonely. Vulnerable.

Had liked the idea of having a father for her son.

Never again would she let down her guard.

Not for any man, no matter what.

DUGAN GATHERED THE fake IDs to investigate them. As much as he wanted to assure her that Lewis had been sincere about his intentions with her, the phony IDs said otherwise.

A liar was a liar, and Dugan hadn't found just one alias. The man had a string of them.

Meaning he probably had a rap sheet, as well, and maybe had committed numerous crimes.

It also opened up a Pandora's box. Any one of the persons he'd conned or lied to might have wanted revenge against him.

The fact that he'd lied to Sage suggested he might have lied to other women. Hell, he might have a slew of girl-friends or wives scattered across Texas. Maybe one in each city where he'd worked or visited.

All with motive, as well.

"Do you know who Lewis met with in town about the new development?"

"George Bates, from the bank," Sage said. "He also met with the town council and talked to several landowners, but I'm not certain which ones or how far he got with them."

"I'll start with Bates." Dugan stuck the envelope of IDs inside his rawhide jacket.

Sage followed him to the door. "Are you going to the sheriff with this?"

Dugan shook his head. "I don't think he'd like me nosing into this, and I don't trust him to find the truth."

"I agree." Sage rubbed her hands up and down her arms, as if to warm herself. The temptation to comfort her pulled at Dugan.

God, she was beautiful. He'd admired her from afar ever since the first time he laid eyes on her. But he'd known then that she was too good for a jaded man like him. She and her little boy deserved a good man who'd take care of them.

And that man wasn't him.

But just because he couldn't have her for himself didn't mean that he wouldn't do right by her. He would take this case.

Because there was the possibility that Benji was alive.

Dugan wouldn't rest until he found him and Sage knew the truth about what had happened two years ago.

Sage caught his arm as he started to leave the room. "Dugan, promise me one thing."

He studied her solemn face. Hated the pain in her eyes. "What?"

"That you won't keep things from me. No matter what you find, I want—I need—to know the truth. I've been lied to too many times already."

He cradled her hand in his and squeezed it, ignoring the heat that shot through him at her touch. "I promise, Sage."

Hell, he wanted to promise more.

But he hurried down the steps to keep himself from becoming like Lewis and telling her what she wanted to hear instead of the truth.

Because the truth was that he had no idea what answers he would find.

SAGE WATCHED DUGAN LEAVE, a sense of trepidation filling her.

At least he was willing to help her look for the answers. But the phony drivers' licenses had shocked her to the core.

How could she have been so gullible when Ron was obviously a professional liar? And now that she knew Ron Lewis wasn't his real name, who was he?

Had he planned to marry her and take care of her and Benji?

No…everything about the man was probably false. He'd obviously fabricated a story to fit his agenda.

But why use her? To worm his way into the town and make residents believe he cared about them, that he was part of them?

Devious. But it made sense in a twisted kind of way.

She straightened the flooring in the closet, then went to Benji's room. Benji had loved jungle animals, so she'd painted a mural of a jungle scene on one wall and painted the other walls a bright blue. She walked over to the shelf above his bed and ran her finger over each of his stuffed animals. *His friends,* he'd called them.

At night he'd pile them all in bed around him, so she could barely find him when she went to tuck him in. His blankie, the one she'd crocheted before he was born, was folded neatly on his pillow, still waiting for his return.

Where was her son? If he'd survived, was he being taken care of? Had someone given him a blanket to sleep with at night and animal *friends* to comfort him in bed?

She thought she'd cried all her tears, but more slipped down her cheeks, her emotions as raw as they were the day she'd discovered that Benji was gone.

The news usually ran stories about missing children. For a few weeks after the car crash, they carried the story about Ron and her son. Although the implication was that both had died in the fire, a request had been made for any information regarding the accident. They'd hoped to find a witness who'd seen the wreck, someone who could tell them if another car had been involved.

But no word had come and eventually other stories had

replaced Benji's on the front page. With this new development, maybe she could arouse the media's interest again.

She hurried downstairs to the kitchen and retrieved the scrapbook with clippings she'd morbidly kept of the crash and the coverage afterward. Why she'd kept them, she didn't know. Maybe she'd hoped one day she'd find something in them that might explain what had happened to Benji.

The small town of Cobra Creek wasn't big enough for a newspaper, but a reporter from Laredo had interviewed her and covered the investigation. At least, what little investigation Sheriff Gandt had instigated.

She noted the reporter's name on the story. Ashlynn Fontaine.

Hoping that the reporter might revive the story and the public's interest, now that Ron's body had been found and that his death was considered a homicide, she decided to call the paper the next morning and speak to Ashlynn.

DUGAN DROVE TO the bank the next day to speak with George Bates, the president. One woman sat at a desk to the left, and a teller was perched behind her station, at a computer.

He paused by the first woman and asked for Bates, and she escorted him to an office down a hallway. A tall, middle-aged man with wiry hair and a suit that looked ten years old shook his hand. "George Bates. You here to open an account?"

Dugan shook his head. "No, sir, I need to ask you some questions about Ron Lewis."

Bates's pudgy face broke into a scowl. "What about him? He's been dead for two years."

"True," Dugan said. "I don't know if you heard, but his body was discovered this morning at Cobra Creek.

It turns out he didn't die in that car crash or fire. He was murdered."

Bates's eyes widened. "What?"

"Yes, he was shot."

Bates rolled his shoulders back in a defensive gesture. "You think I know something about that?"

"That's not what I meant to imply," Dugan said, using a low voice to calm the man. "But the fact that Ms. Freeport's little boy wasn't with him raises questions about where he is. Ms. Freeport asked me to look into his disappearance. Learning who killed Lewis might lead us to that innocent little boy." Dugan paused. "You do want to help find that child, don't you?"

His comment seemed to steal the wind out of Bates's sails. "Well, yes, of course."

"Then tell me everything you can about Ron Lewis."

Bates tugged at his suit jacket, then motioned for Dugan to take a seat.

"Lewis came in here with all kinds of plans for the town," Bates said. "He had sketches of how he wanted to renovate the downtown area, parks that would be added, housing developments, a giant equestrian center and a dude ranch, along with an outlet mall and new storefronts for the downtown area."

"Did he have backing?" Dugan asked.

Bates scratched his chin. "Well, that was the sketchy part. At first he said he did. Then, when it got down to it, he approached me to invest. I think he may have hit on some others around town. Especially Lloyd Riley and Ken Canter. They own a lot of land in the prime spots for the equestrian center and dude ranch."

"He made them offers?"

"You'd have to talk to them about it," Bates said. "Neither one wanted to tell me any specifics. But I think Riley signed something with him and so did Canter."

So, what had happened to those deals?

"Were most of the people in town in favor of the project?"

"A few of the store owners thought it would be good for business. But some old-timers didn't want that dude ranch or the mall."

"When he asked you to invest, did you check out Lewis's financial background?"

Bates frowned. "I was going to, but then he had that crash and I figured there wasn't no need."

"Was he working with a partner? Another contact to deal with on the project?"

"If he was, he didn't tell me."

Probably because he was running a scam. Lewis had never had backing and was going to swindle the locals into investing, then run off with their money.

Had one of them discovered Lewis's plans to cheat him and killed Lewis because of it?

Chapter Five

Dugan stopped by his ranch before heading out to talk to the ranchers Lewis had approached.

He'd worked hard as a kid and teen on other spreads, doing odd jobs and then learning to ride and train horses, and had vowed years ago that he would one day own his own land.

Growing up on the reservation had been tough. His mother was Native American and had barely been able to put food on the table. Like little Benji's, his father had skipped out. He had no idea where the man was now and couldn't care less if he ever met him.

Any man who abandoned his family wasn't worth spit.

Then he'd lost his mother when he was five and had been tossed around for years afterward, in foster care, never really wanted by anyone, never belonging anywhere. It was the one reason he'd wanted his own land, his own place. A home.

He'd hired a young man, Hiram, to help him on the ranch in exchange for a place to live. Hiram was another orphan on the rez who needed a break. He also employed three other teens to help groom and exercise the horses and clean the stalls. Keeping the boys busy and teaching them the satisfaction of hard work would hopefully help them stay out of trouble. He'd also set up college scholarships if they decided to further their education.

Everything at the ranch looked in order, and he spotted Hiram at the stables. He showered and changed into a clean shirt and jeans, then retreated to his home office.

He booted up his computer and researched Trace Lanier. Seconds after he entered the man's name, dozens of articles appeared, all showcasing Lanier's rise in success in the rodeo. Other photos revealed a line of beautiful rodeo groupies on his arm. For the past two years, he'd been traveling the rodeo circuit, enjoying fame and success.

He had no motive for trying to get his son back. He had plenty of money. And now fame. And judging from the pictures of him at honky-tonks, parties and casinos, he enjoyed his single life.

At the time of Benji's disappearance, he was actually competing in Tucson.

Dugan struck Lanier off the suspect list, then phoned his buddy Jaxon and explained about finding Lewis's corpse and the phony identities.

"Sounds like a professional con artist," Jaxon said. "Send me a list of all his IDs and I'll run them."

Dugan typed in the list and emailed it to Jaxon. He could use all the help he could get.

"I'm plugging them in, along with his picture," Jaxon said. "Now, tell me what you know about this man."

"He came to Cobra Creek on the pretense of saving the town. Said he had a developer wanting to rebuild the downtown, and expand with an equestrian center, dude ranch, shopping mall and new storefronts. The banker in town said he approached him to invest and that he solicited locals to, as well. I'm going to question them next. But I'm anxious to learn more about his background. Does he have an arrest record?"

"Jeez. He was a pro."

"What did you find?"

"He stole the name Lewis from a dead man in Corpus Christi."

"A murder victim?"

"No, he was eighty and died of cancer."

"So he stole his identity because it was easy."

"Yeah, Lewis was an outstanding citizen, had no priors. His son died in Afghanistan."

"What else?"

"Three of the names—Joel Bremmer, Mike Martin and Seth Handleman—have rap sheets."

"What for?"

"Bremmer for theft, Martin for fraud and embezzlement and Handleman for similar charges."

"Did he do time for any of the crimes?"

"Not a day. Managed to avoid a trial by jumping bail."

"Then he took on a new identity," Dugan filled in.

"Like I said, he's a pro."

"Who bailed him out?"

"Hang on. Let me see if I can access those records."

"While you're at it, see if you can get a hold of Sheriff Gandt's police report on Lewis's car accident. I want to know if Lewis was shot before the accident or afterward."

"The sheriff doesn't know?"

"According to Gandt, he thought the man died in the car fire. Now we have a body, the M.E. pointed out the gunshot wound. When I asked Gandt if he saw a bullethole in the car, he sidestepped the question, and said the car was burned pretty badly. But all that tells me is that he didn't examine it."

"Shoddy work."

"You could say that."

Dugan drummed his fingers on the desk while he waited. Seconds later, Jaxon returned.

"Each time, a woman bailed him out. The first time, the lady claimed to be his wife. The second, his girlfriend."

"Their names?"

"Eloise Bremmer," Jaxon said. "After Bremmer disappeared, the police went to question her, but she was gone, too. Same thing with Martin's girlfriend, Carol Sue Tinsley."

"Hmm, wonder if they're one and the same."

"That's possible."

"How about the other names?"

"One more popped. Seth Handleman. He was charged with fraud, but the charges were dropped. Says here his wife, Maude, lives in Laredo."

"Give me that address," Dugan said. "Maybe she's still there."

She also might be the same woman who'd bailed out Bremmer and Martin.

SAGE RUBBED HER FINGER over the locket she wore as she parked at the coffee shop where Ashlynn Fontaine had agreed to meet her. After Benji had disappeared, she'd placed his picture inside the necklace and sworn she wouldn't take it off until she found her son.

It was a constant reminder that he was close to her heart even if she had no idea if he was alive or…gone forever.

Clinging to hope, she hurried inside, ordered a latte and found a small corner table to wait. Five minutes later, Ashlynn entered, finding Sage and offering her a small smile. Ashlynn ordered coffee, then joined her, shook off her jacket and dropped a pad and pen on the table.

"Hi, Ms. Freeport. I'm glad you called."

"Call me Sage."

"All right, Sage. You said there's been a new development in the case."

Sage nodded. "I take it you haven't heard about Ron Lewis's body being found."

The reporter's eyes flickered with surprise. "No, but that is news. Who found him?"

"Dugan Graystone, a local tracker, was searching for some missing hikers and discovered his body at Cobra Creek."

"I see. And the sheriff was called?"

Sage nodded. "Sheriff Gandt said he would investigate, but he didn't do much the first go-around."

"How did Lewis die?" Ashlynn asked.

"He was shot."

"Murdered?" Another flicker of surprise. "So he didn't die from an accident?"

"No." Sage ran a hand through her hair. "He died of a gunshot wound. At this point it's unclear if he was shot before the accident, causing him to crash, or after it, when he tried to escape the burning vehicle."

"Interesting."

"The important thing is that they found Lewis's body but not my son's. So Benji might be alive."

Ashlynn gave her a sympathetic look. "Did they find any evidence that he survived?"

"No," Sage admitted. "But they also didn't find any proof that he didn't."

"Fair enough."

"Think about it," Sage said. "The shooter may have wanted to kill Ron. But maybe he didn't realize Ron had Benji with him. When he killed Ron and discovered Benji, he may have taken my son."

A tense heartbeat passed between them, fraught with questions.

"That's possible," Ashlynn said. "But it's also possible that he didn't."

Sage's stomach revolted. "You mean that he got rid of Benji."

"I'm sorry," Ashlynn said. "I don't want to believe that, but if he murdered Lewis, he might not have wanted any witnesses left behind."

Sage desperately clung to hope that Ron's killer hadn't been that inhumane. Killing a grown man for revenge, if that was the case, was a far cry from killing an innocent child.

Ashlynn traced a finger along the rim of her coffee cup. "I hate to suggest this, but did the police search the area for a grave, in case the killer buried your son?"

Sage's throat closed. She clutched her purse, ready to leave. "I didn't call you so you'd convince me that Benji is dead. I hoped you'd run another story, this time focus on the fact that Lewis's body was found but that Benji might still be out there."

She pulled a picture of her son from her shoulder bag. "Please print his picture and remind people that he's still missing. That I'm still looking for him." Desperation tinged her voice. "Maybe someone's seen him and will call in."

Ashlynn reached over and squeezed her hand. "Of course I can do that, Sage. I'll do whatever I can to help you get closure."

Sage heard the doubt in the reporter's voice. She didn't think Benji would be found.

But Sage didn't care what she thought. "I know you have your doubts about him being alive, but I'm his mother." Sage stroked the locket where it lay against her heart. "I can't give up until I know for sure."

Ashlynn nodded and took the picture. "Did Benji have any defining characteristics? A birthmark, scar or mole? Anything that might stand out?"

"As a matter of fact, he does," Sage said. "He was born with an extra piece of cartilage in his right ear. It's not very noticeable, but if you look closely, it almost looks like he has two eardrums."

"Do you have a photo where it's visible?"

Sage had actually avoided photographing it. But it was obvious in his first baby picture. She removed it from her wallet and showed it to Ashlynn.

"This might help," the reporter told her. "I'll enhance it for the news story. And I'll run the story today." Ashlynn finished her coffee. "As a matter of fact, I have a friend who works for the local TV station. I'll give her a heads-up and have her add it to their broadcast. The more people looking for Benji, the better."

Sage thanked her, although Ashlynn's comment about searching for a grave troubled her.

As much as she didn't want to face that possibility, she'd have to ask Dugan about it.

DUGAN ENTERED THE ADDRESS for Maude Handleman into the note section on his phone, then drove toward Lloyd Riley's farm, a few miles outside town.

He'd heard about the tough times some of the landowners had fallen upon in the past few years. Weather affected farming and crops, the organic craze had caused some to rethink their methods and make costly changes, and the beef industry had suffered.

Farmers and ranchers had to be progressive and competitive. He noted the broken fencing along Riley's property, the parched pastures and the lack of crops in the fields.

He drove down the mile drive to the farmhouse, which was run-down, the porch rotting, the paint peeling. A tractor was abandoned in the field, the stables were empty and a battered black pickup truck was parked sideways by the house.

It certainly appeared as if Riley might have been in trouble.

Dugan parked and walked up the porch steps, then knocked. He waited a few minutes, then knocked again, and the sound of man's voice boomed, "Coming!"

Footsteps shuffled, then the door opened and a tall, rangy cowboy pushed the screen door open.

"Lloyd Riley?"

The man tipped his hat back on his head. "You're that Indian who found the hikers?"

"I was looking for them, but another rescue worker actually found them," Dugan said. He offered his hand and Riley shook it.

"Name's Dugan Graystone."

"What are you doing out here?" Riley asked.

Dugan chose his words carefully. Tough cowboys were wary of admitting they had money problems. "I spoke with George Bates at the bank about that development Ron Lewis had planned around Cobra Creek."

Riley stiffened. "What about it?"

"Bates said he asked him to invest before he died. He also mentioned that he talked to some of the locals about investing, as well."

"So?" Riley folded his arms. "He held meetings with the town council and talked to most everyone in town about it. Didn't he approach you?"

Dugan shook his head. "No, he probably meant to, but he didn't get around to me before he died."

Riley pulled at his chin. "Yeah, too bad about that."

The man sounded less than sincere. And Bates had said that he thought Riley made a deal with Lewis. "I heard Lewis offered to buy up some of the property in the area and made offers to landowners. Did he want to buy your farm?"

Riley's eyes flickered with anger. "He offered, but I told him no. This land belonged to my daddy and his daddy.

I'll be damned if I was going to let him turn it into some kind of shopping mall or dude ranch."

"So you refused his offer?"

"Yeah. Damn glad I did. Heard he cheated a couple of the old-timers."

"How so?"

"Offered them a loan to get them out of trouble, supposedly through the backer of this rich development. But fine print told a different story."

"What was in the fine print?"

"I don't know the details, but when it came time to pay up and the guys couldn't make the payments, he foreclosed and stole the property right out from under them."

Riley reached for the door, as if he realized he'd said too much. "Why'd you say you wanted to know about all this?"

"Just curious," Dugan said.

Riley shot him a look of disbelief, so he decided to offer a bone of information.

"Lewis was a con artist," Dugan said. "The day of his so-called accident, I suspect he was running away with the town's money."

Riley made a sound of disgust. "Sounds like it."

"Who was it he swindled?"

"Don't matter now. Lewis is dead."

"Why do you think that?"

"I figured the deal was void when he died. Haven't seen anyone else from that development come around."

That was true. But if they'd signed legal papers, the deal would still be in effect. Unless the paperwork hadn't been completed or whoever killed Lewis had him tear up the papers before Lewis died. "Can you give me a name or two so I can follow up?"

"Listen," Riley said. "These are proud men, Graystone. You know about being proud?"

His comment sounded like a challenge, a reminder

that Riley knew where Dugan had come from and that he should be grateful he'd gotten as far as he had. "Yes, I do."

"Then, they don't want anyone to know they got gypped. Maybe that accident was a blessing."

"I guess it was for some people," Dugan said. "But, Riley, the body I found earlier was Ron Lewis's. He didn't die in an accident."

Riley's sharp angular face went stone-cold. "He didn't?"

"No, he was murdered." Dugan paused a second to let that statement sink in. "And odds are that someone Lewis cheated killed him." Anger hardened Riley's eyes as he realized the implication of Dugan's questions. "What about Ken Canter? Was he one of those Lewis cheated?"

"Canter didn't care about the money. He was just happy to unload his place. He wanted to move near his daughter and took off as soon as he signed with Lewis." Riley made a low sound in his throat. "We're done here."

Riley reached for the door to slam it, but Dugan caught it with the toe of his boot. "I know you want to protect your buddies, but Sage Freeport's three-year-old son disappeared the day Lewis was murdered." He hissed a breath. "Lewis was a con artist, there's no doubt about that. And I'm not particularly interested in catching the person who killed him, *except*—" he emphasized the last word "—except that person may know where Benji is. And if he's alive, Sage Freeport deserves to have her little boy back."

Chapter Six

Sage had slept, curled up with Benji's blanket the night before. Just the scent of him lingering on it gave her comfort.

But Ashlynn's comment about a grave haunted her.

After she arrived back at the B and B, she called Dugan. She explained about her visit with Ashlynn and her suggestion that the sheriff should have looked for a grave where the killer might have buried her son.

"According to the report my friend got for me, the sheriff arrived at the scene shortly after the explosion. I don't think the killer would have had time to dig a hole and bury Benji, but if it'll make you feel better, I'll check it out."

His words soothed her worries, but she couldn't leave any questions unanswered. "Thank you, Dugan. It *would* make me feel better."

"All right. I'll head over there now."

"I'll meet you at the crash site."

She hung up, poured a thermos of coffee to take with her, yanked her unruly hair into a ponytail, then rushed outside to her van.

By the time she arrived, Dugan was waiting. "You didn't have to come, Sage. I could handle this."

"This search should have been done a long time ago."

"Actually, the police report said that searchers did comb the area for Benji after the crash."

She studied Dugan. "Were you part of that team?"

He shook his head, the overly long strands of his dark hair brushing his collar. "I was out of town, working another case."

"I understand it's a long shot, and I hope there isn't a grave," Sage said, "but ever since that reporter suggested it, I can't get the idea out of my head."

"All right." He squeezed her hand, sending a tingle of warmth through her.

She followed him to the spot where the car had crashed and burned. He pulled a flashlight from his pocket and began scanning the ground near the site, looking for anything the police might have missed.

Sage followed behind him, the images of the fire taunting her. She'd imagined them finding Benji's burned body so many times that she felt sick inside.

But they hadn't found him, and that fact gave her the will to keep going.

The next two hours, she and Dugan walked the scene, searching shrubs and bushes, behind rocks, the woods by the creek and along the river and creek bank.

Finally, Dugan turned to her. "He's not here, Sage. If he was, we would have found something by now."

Relief surged through her. "What now?"

"Maybe the news story will trigger someone to call in."

She nodded, and they walked back to their vehicles. "I have a couple of leads to check out," Dugan said. "I found some information on the fake IDs and discovered that at least one of Lewis's aliases was married. I'm driving to Laredo to see if I can talk to the woman."

Sage's stomach lurched. So Ron had not only lied to her but proposed to her when he'd already had a wife.

DUGAN WAS RELIEVED when he didn't discover a grave. Knowing there had been a search team after the crash had suggested the area was clean, but Gandt had led the team and Dugan didn't trust him.

The sheriff had obviously taken the accident at face value and hadn't had forensics study the car, or he might have found a bullet hole and realized the accident wasn't an accident at all. Unless Lewis was shot after he left the burning vehicle...

"Let me go with you to see the woman," Sage said.

Dugan frowned. "If she's covering for her husband, she might not want to talk to us."

"You think she knew what he was doing? That he had other women?"

Dugan shrugged. "Who knows? If he's run the same scam in other cities, she might be his accomplice. Or... she could have been a victim like you were."

"Just a dumb target he used."

"You aren't dumb, Sage," Dugan said. "Judging from the number of aliases this man had, he was a professional, meaning he's fooled a lot of people."

"He also could have made a lot of enemies."

"That, too." More than one person definitely had motive to want him dead.

Sage's keys jangled in her hand. "Follow me back to the inn and then let me ride with you. If she was a victim, then she might talk to me more easily than you."

Dugan couldn't argue with that. "All right."

Ten minutes later, she parked and joined him in his SUV, and he drove toward Laredo. "How did you find out about her?" Sage asked.

"My buddy with the rangers plugged the aliases into the police databases. Lewis had a rap sheet for fraud, money laundering and embezzlement."

"He did time?"

"No. In each instance, a woman bailed him out. Then he disappeared under a new name."

"It sounds like a pattern."

"Yes, it does," Dugan agreed.

Sage leaned her head against her hand. "I still can't believe I was so gullible."

"Let it go, Sage," Dugan said gently.

"How can I? If I hadn't allowed Ron—or whatever his name was—into our lives, Benji wouldn't be gone." Her breath rattled out. "What kind of mother am I?"

Dugan's chest tightened, and he automatically reached for her hand and squeezed it. "You were—are—a wonderful mother. You loved your son and raised him on your own. And my guess is that you never once considered doing anything without thinking of him first."

Sage sighed. "But it wasn't enough. I let Ron get close to us, and he took Benji from me...."

Dugan reminded himself not to let emotions affect him, but he couldn't listen to her berate herself. "I promise you we'll find him, Sage."

Of course, he couldn't promise that Benji would be alive.

Tears glittered in Sage's eyes, but she averted her gaze and turned to stare out the window.

Dugan hated to see her suffering. Still, he gripped the steering wheel and focused on the road, anything to keep himself from pulling over and dragging her up against him to comfort her.

SAGE LATCHED ON to Dugan's strong, confident voice and his promise. He seemed to be the kind of man who kept his word.

But she'd been wrong about men before. Her track record proved that. First Benji's father and then Ron.

No, she was obviously a terrible judge of character.

But this was different. Dugan was known for being

honest and fair and good at what he did. Taking on her case was nothing personal, just a job to him.

She studied the signs and business fronts as they neared Laredo. Dugan veered onto a side street before they entered town and wound through a small modest neighborhood. He checked the GPS and turned right at a corner, then followed the road until it came to a dead end.

A small, wood house with green shutters faced the street. Weeds choked the yard, and a rusted sedan sat in the drive.

"This woman's name is Maude Handleman," Dugan said as they walked up to the front door. He knocked, and she studied the neighboring houses while they waited. If Ron had made money conning people, what had he done with it? He certainly hadn't spent it on this property.

Dugan knocked again, and footsteps pounded, then the sound of a latch turning. The door opened, revealing a short woman with muddy brown hair pulled back by a scarf.

"Mrs. Handleman?" Dugan said.

Her eyes narrowed as she scrutinized them through the screen. "If you're selling something, I don't want it."

"We aren't selling anything," Dugan said. "Please let us come in and we'll explain."

"Explain what?"

Sage offered her a smile. "Please, Maude. It's important. It's about your husband."

The woman's face paled, but she opened the door and let them in. "What has he done now?"

Sage followed Maude inside, with Dugan close behind her. The woman led them into a small den. Sage glanced around in search of family pictures, her pulse hammering when she spotted a photograph of Maude and the man she called Ron Lewis, sitting on the side table.

"All right," Maude said impatiently. "What's this about?"

Dugan glanced at her, and Sage began, "Your husband, what was his name?"

"Seth," Maude said. "Except I haven't seen him since I bailed his butt out of jail nearly four years ago."

"Mrs. Handleman, did you know that Seth has other names that he goes by?"

Surprise flickered in the woman's eyes. "Other names?"

"Yes." Dugan explained about finding the various drivers' licenses. "He has been arrested under at least three assumed names. That's how we found you."

She studied them for a minute. "Who are you—the police come to take him back to jail?"

Sage inhaled a deep breath. "Actually, no. Seth came to Cobra Creek where I live, but he told me and everyone in the town that his name was Ron Lewis."

Maude twisted a piece of hair around one finger.

"He posed as a real estate developer who had big plans for Cobra Creek," Sage continued.

"He did do some real estate work," Maude said.

"He was arrested for fraud and embezzlement," Dugan cut in. "And I believe he was trying to swindle landowners around Cobra Creek."

Maude crossed her arms, her look belligerent. "Look, you can accuse him all you want, but if you want me to pay back whatever he took from folks, I don't have any money." She gestured around the room. "Just look at this. He left me high and dry."

"We don't want your money," Dugan said.

"Then, what do you want?"

Sage sighed softly. "Maude, the day Ron Lewis left Cobra Creek, he took my three-year-old little boy with him."

"He kidnapped your son?" Shock flashed red on Maude's face. "He might have been a cheat, but I find that hard to believe."

Sage nodded. "It's true. He took him from my house. My son's name is Benji." She pulled a photo from her purse and handed it to the woman. "That was taken two years ago. I haven't seen him since."

Maude's alarmed gaze met hers. "I don't understand. Seth…he cheated people out of money, but he wasn't no kidnapper."

Sage's stomach knotted. "I don't know why he took Benji," she said. "But I know that he lied to me. He asked me to marry him, and he warmed up to Benji from the start. Did the two of you have children?"

She shook her head. "I had a miscarriage right after we got married. After that, I was scared to try again."

"Did he talk about children a lot? Did he want a family?"

Maude's lip curled into a scowl. "No."

"What about his own family?" Dugan asked. "Did he tell you anything about them? Did you ever meet his mother or father?"

"No, he said his parents were dead and he didn't have any brothers or sisters."

"When was the last time you saw or talked to him?"

"I told you, right after I bailed him out of jail about four years ago."

"Did he come home with you that night?" Dugan asked.

"Yeah. He spent the night, then said he was going to make things right, that he had to talk to someone about a job and that he'd be back when he got things worked out."

Sage lowered her voice. "Did you have any idea that he'd been arrested before?"

Maude shook her head no.

"How about that he used different names?"

"I told you I didn't know what he was up to."

"He didn't call you and tell you about being in Cobra Creek?" Sage asked.

"No. I… When I didn't hear from him, I was afraid something bad happened to him. That the law caught up with him and he was back in jail."

"So you didn't look for him?" Sage asked.

"I called his cell phone, but it was dead."

"You haven't heard the news, then?" Sage asked.

She crossed her arms, irritation tightening her face. "No, what the hell is going on?"

Sage glanced at Dugan, and he cleared his throat. "I'm sorry to have to tell you, Mrs. Handleman, but Ron Lewis…aka Seth Handleman…was murdered."

Maude gasped and twisted the afghan between her fingers. "What? Who killed him?"

"That's the reason we're here," Dugan said. "I'm investigating his murder."

Sage studied Maude's reaction. She seemed sincerely shocked. And she'd given no indication that she'd killed him or that she wanted him dead.

"Please, Maude, if you can think of a place Seth would have gone or someone he would have contacted, tell me. I'm afraid that whoever killed him took my little boy, and that Benji's in danger."

MAUDE'S FACE PALED. "I…just can't see my Seth kidnapping your boy. If he did, someone must've forced him to."

Dugan had considered that. "But Ms. Freeport didn't receive a ransom note."

Maude threw her hands up. "I don't know what to say except I'm sorry, Ms. Freeport. But I don't know anything."

"Do you recognize the names Mike Martin or Joel Bremmer?" Dugan asked.

"No, should I?"

"They're two of Lewis's other aliases."

Maude dropped her face into her hands. "You think someone he conned killed him?"

"That's possible," Dugan said. "Or it could have been one of the other women in his life."

Maude made a strangled sound. "I shoulda known he wasn't faithful when he left me. Why do I always fall for the losers?"

Sage patted her back with compassion. "I know just how you feel, Maude."

He laid a business card on the table beside her. "Call us if you think of anything."

Sage sighed as they walked outside to the SUV and got inside. "What do we do now?"

"There were two other women on the list I want to question."

"Other wives?"

"One was a wife, one a girlfriend." He fastened his seat belt. "Maybe one of them can shed some light on Lewis. If he lied to Maude about having a family, one of them might know."

"You think if he had family, they might have Benji?"

"I don't know, but there might be some answers in his past that will tell us who killed him."

Chapter Seven

Sage laid her head against the back of the seat and dozed while Dugan drove to the address he had for Mike Martin. According to Jaxon, his girlfriend was named Carol Sue Tinsley. She volunteered at a local women's shelter.

The small town was south of Laredo and took him an hour to reach. Just as he neared the outskirts, Sage cried out, "No, please don't take him...."

Dugan gritted his teeth and realized she was in the throes of a nightmare. How many nights had she actually slept in the past two years without suffering from bad dreams?

"Please..." She choked on a sob.

Dugan gently reached over and pulled her hand into his. "Sage, shh, you're dreaming."

She jerked her eyes open with a start.

"It's okay," he said softly. "A nightmare?"

She blinked as if to focus and straightened as if to shake off the dream, although the remnants of fear and sorrow glittered in her green irises.

He turned into an apartment complex that had seen better days, checking the numbers on the buildings until he reached 10G, Martin's last known address.

A few cars and pickups filled the parking spaces, although there were more empty spaces than those occupied, indicating that the building wasn't filled to capacity. The patios looked unkempt, and overlooked parched land, and the roof of the building needed repairs.

He parked and turned to Sage. "Do you want to wait here?"

"No, let's go."

Together they walked up to the building, then climbed the stairs to the second-floor unit. The cinder-block walls needed painting, and someone had painted graffiti on the doorway to the stairs.

"Ron liked money. He always wore designer suits and drove a nice car." Sage wrapped her arms around her waist. "I can't imagine him living in a place like this."

Dugan silently agreed. Although Mrs. Handleman's home hadn't been in great shape and her house wasn't filled with expensive furnishings, it was upscale compared to these apartments.

"Maybe he and Carol Sue were lying low until he made the big score." And his fancy suits and car were a show to make the ranchers believe he was big, important. That he could save them financially.

It was dark inside.

"No one is here," Sage said.

Dugan tried the door, but it was locked. He removed a small tool from his pocket and picked the lock. The door screeched open, revealing a deserted living area with stained carpet and faded gray walls.

"Stay behind me," Dugan said as he inched inside. He glanced left at the kitchen, then spotted a narrow hallway and paused to listen for sounds that someone was inside. Something skittered across the floor, and Sage clutched his arm. "It sounds like rats."

Dugan nodded, senses alert as he crept closer. There were two bedrooms, both empty. He stepped inside the first one, crossed the room and checked the closet. Nothing.

He and Sage moved to the next one, but when he opened the door, a bird flew across the room, banged into the window and then flew back.

"It's trapped," Sage said.

Dugan closed the distance to the window and opened it, giving the bird a way to escape.

"It looks like whoever lived here has been gone awhile."

Judging from the bird droppings and the musty odor, he agreed. "After I search the apartment, I want to speak to the landlord and find out if they left a forwarding address."

"I saw an office when we first drove in."

Dugan checked the closets, but they were empty. Then he led the way back to the living area. He stepped into the kitchen and searched the drawers and cabinets. "Nothing. And no sign of where she went."

They walked outside and Dugan locked the door. Then they drove to the rental office. Dugan carried a photo of Lewis inside, and a receptionist with big hair and turquoise glasses greeted them. "You folks looking for an apartment?"

If he was, he sure as hell wouldn't spend money at this dump. "No, just some information. Is the landlord here?"

She shook her head. "It's his day off."

Dugan checked her name tag—Rayanne—and faked a smile. "Then maybe you can help us, Rayanne."

She batted blue-shadowed eyes at him. "I'll sure try."

"How long have you worked here?"

She laughed, a flirty sound. "Feels like half my life."

He laid the picture of Ron Lewis on the desk. "Do you recognize this man? He lived in 10G."

She adjusted her glasses and studied the picture. "Well, that looks sort of like Mike Martin. Except he had sandy brown hair and a mustache."

Dugan glanced at Sage, then laid the phony license with Martin's picture on it. "This was him?"

"Yeah, that was Mike." She looked up at him with questioning eyes. "He was a real charmer, although that girlfriend of his was a piece of work."

"How so?" Dugan asked.

"She always ragged on him about this place. Didn't think it was good enough for her."

"Did you know them very well?"

"Naw, he was kind of a flirt. Kept telling me he was gonna make it big one day and then he'd show Carol Sue he was important. That she was wrong about him." She fiddled with her glasses again. "But they've been gone from here a long time. What's this about?"

"Did you know Mike was arrested?" Dugan asked.

Rayanne averted her gaze, a guilty look. "Why are you asking about that?"

"Because he tried to con the people in my town, and he conned me," Sage said. "He also ran off with my little boy and then he was murdered. I'm looking for my son now."

Rayanne's expression went flat. "Well, damn."

"What?" Dugan asked.

"I did hear he was arrested, but I didn't know what it was all about."

"Carol Sue bailed him out of jail after his arrest," Dugan said.

"Yeah," Rayanne muttered. "But the next day, both of them packed up and ran. Skipped out on the rent and left the place in a mess. Mr. Hinley had to hire someone to haul out all their junk."

"What did he do with it?" Dugan asked.

"Took it to that landfill," Rayanne said. "Wasn't anything worth keeping or selling."

Another dead end. "Did Mike ever mention anything about a family? His parents or a sibling?"

Rayanne shook her head.

"How about a friend he might have gone to when he needed a place to stay or hide out?"

Rayanne looked sheepish. "Well…"

"Give us a name," Dugan said.

"He had another woman on the side. Carol Sue didn't know about her, but she lived in 2D. Beverly Vance. She's a hairstylist down at Big Beautiful Hair."

"Does she still live in the complex?" Sage asked.

Rayanne nodded. "But I'd appreciate it if you didn't tell her that I sent you."

"Why not? Don't you two get along?"

Rayanne frowned. "Tarnation, that woman was as jealous as they come. She hated Carol Sue and told me to stay out of her way. Declared she was going to have Mike to herself, one way or the other."

Dugan grimaced. So, he could add Beverly Vance to the growing suspect list.

In fact, any one of the women Lewis had conned and scorned could have killed him.

SAGE SILENTLY PRAYED that Beverly Vance knew something about her son as they walked up to the woman's apartment and knocked. "If Beverly killed Ron…Mike…maybe she took Benji," Sage said.

"That's possible. But Rayanne didn't mention anything about a child living with her."

Sage's mind raced. "Maybe she dropped him at a church or hospital, somewhere where he'd be safe."

"That's possible," Dugan said. "Although when the story aired about Benji being taken by Lewis, if he had been dropped off, someone would have probably notified the authorities."

"Maybe," Sage said. "But maybe not. Especially if they took Benji to another state. And Gandt didn't issue an Amber alert."

Dugan's dark look made Sage's stomach knot.

"Oh, God…what if whoever took him carried him to Mexico?" Then she might never know what happened to him or get him back.

"We can't jump to conclusions," Dugan said. "Let's follow the pieces of the puzzle and see where they lead us."

Sage just hoped they didn't lead to Mexico. Finding Benji in the United States would be difficult enough, but crossing into another country where the legal system was less than satisfactory would complicate matters more.

Dugan knocked again, but no answer, so they walked back to his SUV and drove to the hair salon where Beverly worked.

Big Beautiful Hair was housed in a trailer on the edge of the small town, across from a convenience store called Gas & Go and a liquor store called Last Stop. Several cars were parked out front, a sign painted in neon pink-and-green advertising the big hair Texas women were famous for.

Sage hurried up the steps to the trailer, anxious to speak to Beverly. When she entered, the whir of hair dryers and blow-dryers filled the air, the scent of perm solution and hair dye nearly overwhelming.

There were three workstations, with patrons in various stages of coloring, cutting, highlighting and dying scattered through the long, narrow room. A half dozen bracelets jangled on the arm of the buxom brunette who approached her.

"Can I help you, miss?" She started to examine Sage's unruly hair, but Sage took a step back.

"I need to see Beverly."

The woman shrugged, then turned and called for Beverly. The platinum blonde at the second station glanced over, her sparkling eye shadow glittering beneath the lights. "Yeah?"

Sage crossed the distance to her, while Dugan hung

back. On the ride over, they'd decided Beverly might open up to her before she would to someone investigating the man Beverly apparently loved. "Can we talk for a minute, Beverly?" Sage said in a low voice.

"You don't want a cut and color today?"

"No, I need to ask you some questions about Mike Martin."

Beverly dropped the curling iron she was using and hurried over to Sage. "Mike, good Lord... Now, there's a blast from the past."

"When was the last time you saw him?" Sage asked.

Beverly chewed her bottom lip for a moment before she answered, "About four and a half years ago."

"How was he?" Sage asked.

Beverly tapped one of her three-inch high heels. "Agitated."

"Did he tell you that he'd been arrested?"

Beverly coaxed Sage to the back by the hair dryers. "Yes, but that was a mistake. He said he was going to get it all worked out and then he'd come back for me."

Sage forced a calm to her voice when she wanted to scream at the woman that she'd been a fool to believe anything Mike Martin had said.

Just as *she'd* been a fool to believe Ron Lewis.

"So you knew he was leaving town?"

Beverly nodded. "He said he was due to make a small fortune and then the two of us would get married and buy a house. Maybe even a ranch of our own."

Disgust filled Sage. Ron certainly could be convincing. "Did he say where he was going to make this fortune?"

Beverly leaned in close. "Said he was into a real estate deal with this developer and he was buying up property left and right. He'd already picked out some land for us." She batted her eyes. "I always dreamed about having a big place in the country. Waking up to the sun."

Clearly Beverly had been snowed by Ron's charm. "Then what happened?"

An odd look glimmered in Beverly's eyes. "Then he just disappeared. I tried calling the phone number I had for him but got a recording, saying it was disconnected. I haven't heard from him since."

"What did you think happened to him?" Sage asked.

Tears moistened Beverly's big blue eyes. "I don't know, but I've been scared to death that something bad happened. That his old girlfriend Carol Sue found out our plans and did something crazy."

"What do you mean, crazy?"

Beverly's voice choked. "I mean, like kill him. She was always jealous of me."

"Did Carol Sue own a gun?"

Beverly nodded. "A .38. She was good at shooting, too. Mike said her daddy took her to the shooting range every week when she was a kid. That she won the skeet-shooting contest at the county fair three years in a row."

Sage dug her nails into the palms of her hands. They had to find Carol Sue. If she'd shot Lewis, maybe she knew where Benji was.

DUGAN SAW THE FRUSTRATION on Sage's face as they left Big Beautiful Hair and drove toward Cobra Creek. Beverly had been completely in love with Mike Martin, aka Ron Lewis.

Dammit, he needed the man's real name. Learning the truth about his upbringing might explain what had shaped him into a con artist. A man who not only swindled people out of their money, but charmed women into believing and trusting him when he told them nothing but lies.

Sage lapsed into silence until they neared the outskirts of Cobra Creek.

"I almost feel sorry for Beverly," Sage said. "She really thought he was coming back to her."

Dugan winced. "He fooled her like he did everyone else."

"Like he did me." Sage's tone reeked of self-disgust. "The minute I realized he took Benji with him, without asking me, I was done with the man. He knew how protective I was of my son. Even if he had simply gone shopping, like I thought at first, I would have been furious." Her voice gained momentum. "You just don't do that to a mother."

Dugan agreed.

"If Beverly was right about Carol Sue, and she shot Ron, what did she do with Benji?"

"I'm going to call Jaxon and ask him to search hospital and church records nationwide for any child who might have been abandoned or dropped off around that time."

"That should have been done two years ago."

"I agree," Dugan said, his opinion of the sheriff growing lower by the minute. Gandt should have explored every avenue to find Benji.

"But if Carol Sue dropped him off, surely Benji would have told someone his name."

A dozen different scenarios ran through Dugan's mind. Not if he was injured, confused, or traumatized. Or if she'd threatened him.

But he tempered his response so as not to panic Sage. "If Carol Sue did leave him, she might have given false information, signed him in using a different name."

"You're right," Sage said. "The woman could have claimed he was her child, given a fake name and said she was coming back for him."

Dugan nodded. "I'll call Jaxon now."

His phone buzzed just as he reached for it, but suddenly

a car raced up behind them and a gunshot blasted the air, shattering the back window.

Sage screamed, and he swerved and pushed her head down, then checked his rearview mirror as the car sped up and slammed into their side.

Chapter Eight

Sage screamed as a bullet pinged off the back of the SUV. Dugan swerved sideways and sped up, but the car behind them roared up on their tail.

"Stay down!" Dugan shouted.

Sage ducked, clutching the seat edge as Dugan veered to the right on a side road. The SUV bounced over ruts in the asphalt, swaying as he accelerated. Suddenly he spun the car around in the opposite direction, tires squealing as he raced back onto the main road.

"What's happening?" Sage cried.

"I'm chasing the bastard now."

Sage lifted her head and spotted a black sedan peeling off and getting farther and farther way. "Who is it?"

"I didn't see his face." He pressed the gas to the floor and tried to catch the car, but they rounded a curve and the driver began to weave.

Dugan closed the distance, pulled his gun and shot at the sedan's tires. The car screeched to the right, skidded and spun, then flipped over and rolled. Metal scrunched and glass shattered as it skated into a boulder.

A second later, the car burst into flames.

Dugan yanked the wheel to the left to avoid crashing into it, then swung the SUV to the side of the road and threw it into Park.

Then he jumped out and ran toward the burning vehicle. Déjà vu struck Sage, images of flames shooting from Ron's car two years ago pummeling her.

That night she'd been terrified Benji had been inside the car.

Today…the driver had shot at them. Tried to kill them. Why? Because she was asking questions about Benji?

She jerked herself from her immobilized state and climbed out. Dugan circled the car, peering in the window as if looking for a way to get the driver out. But the gas tank blew, another explosion sounded and flames engulfed the vehicle.

Sweat beaded on her forehead, the heat scalding her. She backed away, hugging the side of the SUV as she watched Dugan. He must have realized it was impossible to save the driver, because he strode back toward her, his expression grim.

"Did you see who it was?"

"A man. I didn't recognize him." Dugan punched a number into his phone. "Jaxon, it's Dugan. I want you to run a plate for me."

Dugan recited the license number, then ran a hand through his hair while he waited.

"Who?" A pause. "No, send a crime team. He's dead, but maybe they can find some evidence from the car."

When he hung up, Sage asked, "Who did the car belong to?"

"Registered to a man named Joel Bremmer."

"Bremmer?"

Dugan nodded. "One of Ron Lewis's aliases."

Sage gasped. "But Ron is dead, so he couldn't have been driving the car."

Questions darkened Dugan's eyes. "I know. The M.E. will work on ID once he gets him to the morgue."

Sage gritted her teeth. "Do you think he was working with Ron?"

"That's possible." Dugan traced his thumb under her chin. "Are you okay?"

She nodded, although she was trembling. Heat reddened his face, the scent of smoke and hot metal permeating him.

"Someone doesn't like us asking questions, Sage. But that means we might be on the right track to finding some answers."

Dugan's gruff voice wrapped around her just as his arms did, and for the first time in two years, she allowed herself to lean on another man.

DUGAN STROKED SAGE'S BACK, soothing her with soft, non-sensical words.

Whoever the bastard was driving the car—he had almost killed them. An inch or two to the right, and that bullet would have pierced Sage's skull.

Cold fear and rage made him burn as hot as the fire consuming the shooter's car.

If Sage had died...

No, she was fine. So was he. And he wasn't going to stop until he unearthed the truth. The fact that someone had shot at them meant he was on the right path. That someone was afraid he'd find Lewis's killer and Benji.

A siren wailed, and Dugan released Sage. "Are you all right now?"

She nodded and tucked a strand of hair behind her ear. "Yes, thanks, Dugan."

Blue lights twirled as the sheriff's car and a fire engine careened toward them. The fire truck screeched to a stop, three firemen jumping down along with a female firefighter who'd been driving.

They rushed to extinguish the blaze while Sheriff Gandt lumbered toward them. "What happened?"

Dugan explained, "The car ran up on us, and the driver shot at us." He pointed out the bullet hole in the back of his SUV. "I swerved to avoid him and he sped past. Then I turned around and tried to catch him, but he lost control and crashed."

Gandt scowled as he looked from Dugan to Sage. "He just come up and shot at you, out of the blue?"

Dugan choked back an obscenity. Gandt was the sheriff and he had to cooperate. If he didn't, the jerk would probably lock him up and then he couldn't find the truth. But he didn't like it. "Yes."

"You've been asking questions about Lewis?"

Dugan nodded. "Turns out Ron Lewis had a few other names he went by," he said. "Then again, I'm sure you already know that."

A cutting look deepened the sheriff's eyes. "Of course. I am the sheriff."

"Right. Have you made any progress on solving his murder?"

"I'm working on it," Sheriff Gandt said, "which means you need to stay out of my investigation."

Sage spoke up. "We're just trying to find my son."

"Right." This time Sheriff Gandt's tone was sarcastic.

A crime van rolled up, interrupting them, and Gandt's mouth twitched with irritation.

"You called them?"

Dugan nodded. "I figured I'd save you the time."

The van parked, and two CSIs exited the vehicle and approached them.

Gandt crossed his beefy arms. "If you know something, spit it out, Dugan. Because if I find out you're holding back, I'll haul your butt in for interfering with a homicide investigation."

Dugan gritted his teeth. The hell he would. "I've told you all I know." He gestured toward the charred remains of the sedan. "Tell me when you identify the driver. I'd like to know who tried to kill me."

Gandt's steely gaze met Dugan's, a challenge in his expression. "Sure thing. After all, I was elected to serve and protect."

Dugan bit back a surly remark, took Sage's arm and they walked back to his SUV. He had a feeling Gandt would have handed the shooter a gun if it meant getting Dugan out of his hair.

But he'd survived a rough childhood, taunts about being a half-breed, other taunts about being a bastard kid. And then the fights as a teenager, when he'd defended himself.

Gandt couldn't intimidate him into doing anything. In fact, his obstinacy only fueled Dugan's drive to get to the bottom of Ron Lewis's murder.

His phone buzzed, and he checked the number. George Bates at the bank.

Sage slipped into the passenger seat, her expression troubled as she watched the firefighters finishing up.

He took the call. "Dugan Graystone."

"Listen, Mr. Graystone, after you left the other day, I got to thinking about Lewis and that development and looked back into some foreclosures. Worst part of my job, but sometimes I don't have a choice."

"Go on."

"There were two that troubled me. Two ranchers I threatened foreclosure on, but they paid me off at the last minute. When I asked how they came up with the money, neither one wanted to tell me. They just said they'd had a streak of luck."

"How so?"

"In both cases, the ranchers were in bad trouble financially. I think they worked out some kind of deal with Lewis, that he offered to pay off their debt by loaning them money from his own company."

Money that he might have earned through another scam. "What happened?"

"One of the men came to me complaining that when he got behind on the payments, Lewis took over his property. Said something about he hadn't read the fine print."

Dammit. That fit with what Lloyd Riley had told him. If Lewis had a large party interested in paying big bucks for the property once he took control of it, Lewis could have turned a big profit by picking it up at foreclosure prices and then reselling.

And Lewis would have given the men he'd conned motive for wanting him dead.

"When Lewis disappeared, the ranchers asked me to keep it quiet that they'd been cheated."

A strong motive to convince Bates not to go public, to void the deal. Although technically, they would have had to go through legal channels, fill out paperwork, and look at Lewis's will, if he had one.

"Which ranchers wanted the deal covered up?"

"I don't want my name mentioned," Bates said. "Bank transactions are supposed to be confidential. If folks think I talk about their private business, they'll quit coming to me."

"I understand. Just give me the names."

"Donnell Earnest," Bates said. "And the other man was Wilbur Rankins."

"Where are they now?"

"Both are still here. When Lewis died, they refused to move, said they had reason to believe the deals weren't legal. That they had a ninety day window that hadn't passed. And so far no one has come forward to uphold the contracts they signed."

Suspicious in itself. If Lewis had investors or a legitimate corporation, someone would follow up on the deals.

Dugan thanked Bates, then made a mental note to talk to both Earnest and Rankins.

He punched Jaxon's number as he started the engine and pulled back onto the road. He asked Jaxon to research children, specifically three-year-old boys, who were left at churches, orphanages, hospitals or women's shelters around the date Benji disappeared.

"Also find out everything you can on these names. Martin's girlfriend, Carol Sue Tinsley. Handleman's wife, Maude. And a woman named Beverly Vance. Any one of them could have killed Lewis."

Jaxon agreed to call him with whatever he learned and then Dugan headed toward Donnell Earnest's ranch outside Cobra Creek.

SAGE'S NERVES FLUTTERED. "You know, Carol Sue could have just run off with Benji. Or since she volunteered at a shelter, what if she faked spousal abuse to get help, then left Benji at one of those women's shelters. From there, they could have disappeared and we may never find them. Carol Sue could have changed their names a dozen times by now."

"Those groups do have underground organizations to help women escape abusive relationships," Dugan agreed. "But we have no real reason to suspect that Carol Sue took him. She may have just freaked out when Martin was arrested and decided to skip town in case she was collared as an accomplice."

"Or she could be dead, too," Sage suggested.

"Maybe. Hopefully Jaxon will find something on her."

Another frightening scenario hit Sage. "What if Benji was hurt or in shock? If he was in that crash or witnessed the shooting, he could have been too traumatized or terrified to talk." Or the shooter could have killed him so there would be no witness left behind.

God…

Dugan squeezed her hand. "I know it's hard not to imagine the worst that could happen, but Benji's age could have worked to his advantage. Toddlers and young children don't make reliable witnesses. And killing a child takes a certain brand of cold-bloodedness that most people don't possess."

"You sound like you have a trusting nature," Sage said wryly.

Dugan made a low sound in his throat. "Not hardly. But I think the fact that we haven't found Benji may be a good sign that he's alive."

Sage tried to mentally hang on to his words.

It was all she had. Besides, she wasn't ready to give up. She never would be.

DUGAN REFUSED TO SPECULATE with Sage, because all the scenarios she mentioned were possible and dwelling on them wouldn't do anything but frighten her more. God knows he'd seen his share of bad outcomes. He'd even met a couple of men he'd called sociopaths.

But intentionally taking the life of a toddler… That was a different breed. A sociopath, maybe.

He was banking on the fact that Lewis's killer wasn't one of them.

Sage's comment about Carol Sue triggered questions.

What if the woman had abducted Benji? If she was aware of Ron's various identities, she might have adopted another name and be living somewhere, raising Benji as her own son.

He phoned Jaxon and asked him to look into that angle and to talk to the people at the shelter where Carol Sue volunteered.

Meanwhile he wanted to check out some of Ron's

aliases. Maybe he'd get lucky and find one of them was still active.

He reached the drive for Donnell Earnest's ranch, the Wagonwheel. Dugan turned the SUV down the dirt drive and drove past several barns and a horse stable. Donnell raised beef cattle, but Dugan saw very few cattle grazing in the pasture.

He parked in front of an ancient farmhouse. Live oaks spread across the dry lawn.

"What's his story?" Sage asked as they climbed out.

"Apparently Donnell Earnest was in trouble financially. Lewis offered the man a loan to help him pay off his bills, but when he fell behind, Lewis took ownership of his ranch. Bates said that no one has come forward from Lewis's company about the deal, and that there was a ninety day window that hadn't passed before Lewis died, so the ranchers think the deal wasn't legal." He paused. "Of course, with Lewis's phony ID, they would have had reason to question the legality anyway."

"*If* they'd discovered he was using an alias," Sage pointed out.

True.

A scrawny beagle greeted them by sniffing his boots and Sage's leg. She bent to pet him, and Dugan walked up the rickety stairs.

Before he could knock, a heavyset guy with a thick dark beard appeared at the screened door, a shotgun in his hand.

"Get off my property or I'll shoot!" Donnell shouted.

"The hit was botched. Graystone and the Freeport woman are still alive."

"Dammit to hell and back. That body washing up at the creek was a big mistake."

"You don't have to tell me that. But the guy deserved to die."

"That's not the point. The point is that I don't want to go to jail."

"Don't worry. They'll never know what happened that day."

"You swear. Because that Freeport woman is about the most persistent woman I've ever known."

"I told you not to sweat it." He'd take care of her if he had to.

They'd come too far to get caught now.

Chapter Nine

"Listen, Mr. Earnest," Dugan said. "I need to ask you some questions about the deal you made with Ron Lewis."

"That's none of your business," Earnest growled.

Dugan gently eased Sage behind him. "I know he cheated you and I don't care. I'm trying to help Ms. Freeport find her little boy. He disappeared the day Lewis did, and his mother misses him."

"I do." Sage stepped up beside Dugan. "I just want to find him, Mr. Earnest. He's probably scared, and he doesn't understand what happened to him."

Donnell waved the gun in front of the screen door. "What makes you think I know something about your kid?"

Sage started to walk forward, but Dugan caught her arm. "Careful. Stay back."

But Sage ignored him. "I know you don't have Benji," Sage said. "But I know Ron Lewis conned you out of your property."

"This land is mine!" Donnell bellowed.

"Yes, it is. Ron Lewis was not the man's real name," Dugan said. "He had several aliases and used them to swindle others besides you."

"You mean that deal was no good?"

"It's not legal," Dugan said, hoping to gain the man's trust. "The lawyers and bank will have to sort out the details."

The big man seemed to relax and lowered his gun. "That's good news, then."

"Except that Ron Lewis's body was found at Cobra Creek. He's dead. In fact, he died the same day of that car crash."

A moment of silence stretched between them. Then Earnest raised the gun again. "So you're here 'cause you think I killed Lewis?"

"I didn't say that. I'm talking to everyone who knew Lewis in hopes that someone Lewis knew or something Lewis said might lead us to Benji."

"I don't know anything and I didn't kill him," Donnell said. "But I'm not sorry the guy's dead."

Dugan started to speak, but Sage cut him off. "I understand, Mr. Earnest. All I want is to find my son. Did Ron mention someone he might meet up with once he left Cobra Creek? Or maybe he had a partner?"

The man lowered the gun, opened the screen and stepped onto the porch. "Naw. He talked about that developer that was going to make Cobra Creek big on the map."

"Was there a contact person or address on any of the papers you signed?"

Donnell scratched his head, sending hanks of hair askew. "Don't recall one." His voice cracked. "I can't believe I was such a damn fool. My mama always said if something was too good to be true, it probably was."

"He fooled a lot of us, Donnell," Sage said sympathetically.

A blush stained his cheeks. "Downright embarrassing to know I was stupid enough to let that jerk steal my land out from under me. Hell, if a man don't have land, he don't have anything."

"Did Ron ever talk about a family?" Dugan pressed. "Did he have parents?"

"Don't remember no folks." The big man rubbed the back of his neck. "Seems like he said he grew up near San Antonio. Or maybe it was Laredo. I think he mentioned a sister once."

"Did he mention her name?"

The dog nuzzled up to his leg, and Donnell scratched him behind the ears. "Janet or Janelle, something like that."

"Thanks," Dugan said. "That might be helpful."

In fact, he'd have Jaxon run the name through the system, along with all of his aliases. Maybe one of them would pop.

"Do you think Mr. Earnest killed Ron?" Sage asked as they left the ranch.

"It's too soon to say. He seems to be telling the truth, but he has motive."

"So do some of the other ranchers." Sage studied the withered grass in the empty pastures, and the stable that looked empty. "But he did seem surprised that Ron was murdered."

"People can fake reactions," Dugan said. "Maybe he was just surprised that we found the body. After two years, whoever killed Lewis had probably gotten complacent. Thought he'd gotten away with murder."

Sage fought despair. Two years a murderer had gone free.

Two years Benji had been gone.

Children changed every day. He would have lost any baby fat from his toddler shape, would have grown taller, more agile. Had the person who'd abducted him been good to him? Was he eating right?

Who tucked him in at night and chased the bogey-man away?

Benji had been afraid of the dark. She'd bought a cartoon-figure night-light and plugged it in before he went to bed. Still, he'd been scared of monsters, so they'd played a game where she checked under the bed and the closets in a big show that she'd chased them away before she kissed him good-night.

Tears pricked her eyes.

At five, he would have started kindergarten this year. She would have already taught him to recognize the letters of the alphabet, and he could count to twenty. Was he learning to read now? Could he write his name?

A dozen more questions nagged at her, but the idea of Benji being in school kept returning. "Dugan, Benji would be five now. He might be in school somewhere. In kindergarten."

Dugan slanted her a sideways look. "That would be risky for the person he's with."

"I suppose you're right. The kidnapper could be home-schooling him." Or locking him in a room and leaving him there alone and afraid.

"Then again, you made a good point. If the person who has Benji is working, he might need for him to be in day care or school." Dugan reached for his phone again. "And it's another place to check out."

He punched in a number and spoke to his friend Jaxon, then asked him to hunt for a Janet or Janelle who might be Lewis's sister. "Make sure the photo of Benji Freeport is circulated to all the school systems in Texas and the surrounding states. Also try day cares."

Sage's heart pounded as Dugan hung up. "Thank you, Dugan."

"I haven't done anything yet," he said in a self-deprecating voice.

"Yes, you have." Sage swallowed the knot in her throat. "You're looking for him and exploring avenues the sheriff never did."

Dugan's gaze met hers, a guarded look in his eyes. "He should have done all this two years ago."

"I know. But he just assumed Benji was dead and told me to accept it and move on." She twisted her fingers in her lap. "But I couldn't do that, Dugan. Not without knowing for sure."

And maybe not even then. Because Benji had been her life. And if he was dead, it was her fault for getting involved with Ron Lewis.

An image of Benji writing his name flashed behind her eyes, and she battled another onslaught of despair as stories of other kidnappings on the news blared in her mind.

Stories where children had been brainwashed, told that their real parents didn't want them, that they'd given them away. Stories where a boy was forced to dress like a girl or vice versa. Stories where children were abducted at such a young age that they adapted to the kidnapper and accepted, even believed, that that person was their real parent.

She couldn't fight the reality that whoever had taken her son had most likely changed his name. That they weren't even calling him Benji anymore.

That the name he might be writing wasn't his own, which would make it even more difficult for a teacher or caretaker to realize that he'd been abducted.

That even if someone asked Benji his name, he might not remember it.

He might not remember her, either, or that she'd once held him in her arms as a baby and rocked him to sleep. That she'd sung him lullabies and chased the bogeyman away and promised to protect him forever.

That she'd dreamed about what he'd become when he grew up.

God…she'd jeopardized her son's life by trusting Ron.

And now she might never see him again.

DUGAN DROVE TO Wilbur Rankins's ranch next. Both Rankins and Earnest had reasons to want Lewis dead.

And they were the only two that Dugan knew of at this point. There could be others. People he'd swindled, along with ex-wives and girlfriends.

The man had been a real class act.

Sage had lapsed into silence. No telling what she was imagining. He wished he could keep her mind from going to the dark places, but that was impossible.

He couldn't even keep his own mind from traveling down those roads.

Rankins's property was fifteen miles outside town and just as run-down as Donnell Earnest's. Both ranchers had probably been desperate and had fallen for Lewis's easy way out.

Dugan pulled up in front of the sprawling ranch house, bracing himself for another hostile encounter. "Stay here until I see if this guy is armed."

Sage nodded. "Okay, but I want to talk to him."

"Sure, once I make sure it's safe." He'd be foolish to let her go in without assessing the situation first. If Donnell had wanted, he could have blown their heads off before they'd even made it onto the porch.

He checked his weapon, then strode up the stone path to the front door. A rusted pickup sat to the left of the house, beneath a makeshift carport. He spotted a teenage boy out back, chopping wood.

Smoke curled from the chimney, and a Christmas tree stood in view, in the front window. He knocked, scanning the property and noting a few head of cattle in the west pasture. Maybe Rankins was getting back on top of his business.

He knocked again, and the door was finally opened. A man who looked to be mid-forties stood on the other side, his craggy face crunched into a frown. "Yeah?"

"Are you Wilbur Rankins?"

"Naw, that'd be my daddy. I'm Junior."

"Is your father here?"

"He's not feeling too good." The man crossed his arms, his tattered T-shirt stretching across his belly. "Who are you and what do you want with him?"

He heard the SUV door open and glanced back to see Sage emerge from the passenger side. He motioned that it was okay for her to join him.

"What's going on?"

Dugan explained who he was and introduced Sage.

"We know that Ron Lewis swindled you," Dugan said. "That you're not the only one."

"I heard he was murdered," Junior Rankins said. "But if you think I did it, think again. I didn't know he'd conned my daddy out of his ranch until after the creep had that car crash."

"Did you meet him yourself?" Sage asked.

Junior shook his head no. "My boy out there and I lived in Corpus Christi at the time. We came down a few months ago when my father took ill."

"I'm sorry," Sage said. "Is it serious?"

"Cancer. He's been fighting it about three years. That's when he started letting things go around here."

"And Lewis popped in to save the day," Dugan guessed.

A disgusted look darkened the man's eyes. "Yeah, damn vulture if you ask me."

Footsteps sounded behind the man, and Dugan saw an older man in a robe appear. *Must be the father.*

"What's going on?" the man bellowed.

Junior turned to his father. "Everything's under control, Dad."

"Mr. Rankins," Dugan said. "Can we talk for a minute?"

The old man shuffled up beside his son and motioned for them to come in. "What the hell's going on? A man can't get any rest."

"I'm sorry," Junior said. "I was trying to take care of it."

The older man looked hollow-eyed, pale, and he'd lost his hair. "Take care of what?"

Dugan cleared his throat and introduced himself and Sage again.

"Mr. Rankins," Sage interjected. "We know that Ron Lewis tried to con you out of your land. But the morning he was leaving town, he took my little boy with him. If you know anything about where he might have been going or who he was working with, please tell me. It might help me find my son."

"I don't know a damned thing." The man broke into a coughing spell. "But I'm glad that bastard's dead so he can't cheat anyone else."

"Where were you the morning he disappeared two years ago?" Dugan asked.

Junior stepped in front of his father. "You don't have to answer that, Dad." Junior shot daggers at Dugan with his eyes. "Now, I suggest you leave before I call the sheriff and tell him you're harassing us."

Dugan was about to make a retort, but his phone buzzed. Surprisingly, Sheriff Gandt's name flashed on his caller ID display. "Graystone speaking."

"Is Sage Freeport with you?"

Dugan said yes through gritted teeth. "Why?"

"Bring her to my office. I have something to show her."

"What?"

"Something that got overlooked after the crime scene workers searched the crash site."

"We'll be right there."

Dugan ended the call, an anxious feeling in his gut. Did Gandt have bad news about Benji?

SAGE'S HANDS FELT clammy as she and Dugan parked at the sheriff's office. Dugan said the sheriff was cryptic about the reason he'd asked them to stop by.

But it couldn't be good news or else he would have told Dugan over the phone.

She reminded herself that she had survived the past two years living in the dark, that she needed closure, no matter what the outcome was.

But she'd be lying if she didn't admit that finding Ron's body and not Benji's had rekindled her hope.

Dugan opened the door to the sheriff's office and gestured for her to enter first. She did, her insides trembling as the sheriff looked up at them from the front desk, his expression grim.

"Sheriff?" Dugan said as they approached.

Sheriff Gandt stood. "After we found Lewis's body, I decided to look back at the evidence box we collected two years ago after the original accident."

"You found something?" Sage asked, her voice a painful whisper.

He nodded. "This envelope was in the bottom of the box stuck under the flap." He opened it and removed a blue whistle.

Sage gasped. The whistle was Benji's.

And it had blood on it.

Chapter Ten

Sage sagged against the desk, then stumbled into a nearby chair. "That was my son's."

"Did you test the blood to see if it belonged to Benji?" Dugan asked.

"Not yet. I wanted to show it to Ms. Freeport first and see if she recognized it."

Sage struggled to pull herself together.

"Get it tested," Dugan said firmly. "It may be Benji's blood. But blood from the person who shot Lewis might also be on it."

"Did you find anything else?" Sage said in a choked voice.

"That's it," Gandt said.

"What about on the man who tried to shoot us?"

"M.E. has him at the morgue now." He gave Dugan a warning look. "Why don't you take Ms. Freeport home and let me do my job? I've got this investigation under control."

Sage bit her tongue to keep from lashing out and telling him that Dugan had already accomplished more in two days on the case than Gandt had in two years.

But arguing with the sheriff was pointless.

She gestured toward the whistle. "After you finish with that, I'd like to have it back."

"Of course."

"You'll let me know what you find?" Sage asked.

His eyes narrowed, but he offered her a saccharine smile. "Sure. And know this, Ms. Freeport, I'm doing everything I can to find Lewis's killer and your son."

"I appreciate that," Sage said, grateful her voice didn't crack. She wanted out of the room, away from Sheriff Gandt.

Away from that whistle with the blood on it, blood that might belong to her son.

DUGAN DROVE SAGE back to the B and B, well aware she'd hit an emotional wall that could crumble any second.

The big question was if she would be able to put herself back together again if she received bad news.

So far, she had held it together. Shown amazing strength and fortitude. But she also had held on to hope.

Damn. She was stubborn, beautiful and fragile and in need of something to turn the nightmare she'd been stuck in the past two years into a distant dream where her son emerged at the end, safe and back at home with her where he belonged.

Dugan walked her up to the door of the inn. "Sage, even if that whistle has Benji's blood on it, it doesn't mean that he's dead."

She winced, and he berated himself for being so blunt. But she had made him promise to be honest with her.

"I know. And I appreciate all you're doing." Her phone beeped that she had a text, and she pulled it from her purse.

"What is it?"

"I talked to that reporter, Ashlynn Fontaine. Not only is she running the story in the newspaper, but she said the story is airing on the news."

Dugan gritted his teeth. The media could be a double-edged sword.

"You think I shouldn't have contacted her?"

He hadn't realized his expression was so transparent. "I didn't say that."

"But?"

Dugan squeezed her arm, aching to do more. To pull her in his arms and promise her he'd fix all her problems and make her happy again.

But the only way to do that was to bring her son home.

"The more exposure Benji's story receives, the more chances are that someone might recognize him."

"That's what I thought."

Dugan lowered his voice. "But be prepared, Sage. It also may bring false leads. And letting everyone know the case has been reopened could be dangerous."

"Someone already shot at us," Sage said. "And just because it's dangerous doesn't mean I'll stop looking." She gripped his hands. "Dugan, I will never give up, not as long as I know there's a chance Benji's out there."

Dugan had heard of kidnapping cases and missing children that spanned decades. He honestly didn't know how the parents survived. They had to live hollow shells of their lives, going through each day on empty hope, like a car running on gas fumes.

"Call me if you hear from your contacts," Sage said. "I'm going inside now."

Dugan nodded, his chest constricting. He hated to leave her alone. But he had work to do.

He needed to track down that woman named Janet or Janelle, Lewis's alleged sister.

Perhaps Lewis had planned to make his fortune in Cobra Creek and then convince Sage to disappear with him. If so, he might have told a sibling about her.

And he might have asked her to watch Benji until he could clean up the mess and return for Sage.

It was a long shot, but Dugan couldn't dismiss any theory at this point.

SAGE WALKED THROUGH the empty B and B, hating the silence. The couple renting from her had gone home to be with their family for the holidays.

Just where they should be.

But the quiet only reminded her that she would spend another Christmas in this house by herself. When she first bought the place and renovated it, she'd imagined a constant barrage of people in and out, filling the rooms with laughter and chatter. She'd spend her days baking her specialty pastries and pies, with Benji helping her, stirring and measuring ingredients and licking icing from the bowl, his favorite part.

Ron must have picked up on that dream and played her. Although she'd wanted a houseful of people because she'd been without family for so long, he'd obviously thought she'd wanted the place to be a success so she could make money.

She glanced in the fridge and pulled out a platter of leftover turkey and made herself a sandwich. Although she had no appetite, she'd forced herself to eat at least one meal a day for the past two years, telling herself that she had to keep up her strength for when she brought her son home.

Would that ever happen?

She poured a glass of milk and took it and the sandwich to the table and turned on the TV to watch the news report.

An attractive blonde reporter, who identified herself as March Williams, introduced the story by showing a picture of Ron Lewis. She recapped the details of the accident two years ago.

"Police now know that Lewis was an alias, and that he was wanted on other charges across the state. They also know he was murdered and are searching for his killer." She paused for dramatic effect. "But another important question remains—where is little Benji Freeport?" A photograph of Benji appeared, making Sage's heart melt.

"Three-year-old Benji Freeport lived with his mother, Sage Freeport, who owns a bed and breakfast in Cobra Creek. The morning Lewis disappeared, he took Benji with him. Police have no leads at this time but are hopeful that Benji is safe and still alive. If you have any information regarding this case or the whereabouts of Benji Freeport, please call the tip line listed on the screen."

Sage glanced at the Christmas tree and Benji's present waiting for him. Each year she'd added another present. How big would the pile get before he came back to open them?

The treetop star lay in the box to the side, taunting her. She had opted not to hang the star, because that was Benji's job.

Battling tears, she folded her hands, closed her eyes and said a prayer that someone would recognize Benji and call the police.

That this year he could hang the star for Christmas and they'd celebrate his homecoming together.

DUGAN STOPPED AT the diner and ordered the meat loaf special. He'd learned to cook on the open fire as a boy on the rez, but he'd never quite mastered the oven or grocery shopping.

Food was meant for sustenance, a necessity to give him the energy to tackle his job. Manning the ranch meant early mornings and manual labor, both of which he liked. It helped him pass the days and kept him busy enough not to think about being alone.

Not that being alone had ever bothered him before. But seeing Sage and the way she loved her son reminded him of the way his mother had loved him before she died.

And the way he'd felt when he was shuffled from foster home to foster home where no one really wanted him.

What had Lewis told Benji the day he abducted him? Where was he now?

He knew the questions Sage was asking herself, because they nagged at him.

Two old-timers loped in, grumbling about the weather and their crops. An elderly man and woman held hands as they slid into a booth.

Sheriff Gandt sat in a back booth, chowing down on a blood-red steak.

Donnell Earnest loped in, claimed a bar stool, removed his hat and ordered a beer.

Nadine, the waitress behind the counter, grinned at him. "Hey, Donnie, you all right?"

"Hell, no, that Indian guy was out asking questions about my business."

Nadine glanced at Dugan over Donnell's shoulder. "I heard he's looking for Sage Freeport's kid."

"Yeah, and Ron Lewis's killer. Son of a bitch deserved what he got."

"I hear you there," Nadine murmured.

Donnell rubbed a hand across his head. "Rankins called me, said Graystone was out there bothering him. That guy starts trying to pin Lewis's murder on one of us, we gotta teach him a lesson."

Dugan rolled his hands into fists to control his temper. The jerk was just venting. God knows, he'd heard worse.

Still, the names and prejudice stung.

The one woman he'd been involved with years ago had received the brunt of more than one attack on him by idiots and their prejudice. She'd broken it off, saying he wasn't worth it.

His daddy had obviously felt the same way.

He'd decided that day that his land and work were all that mattered.

A cell phone rang from the back. Then the sheriff

jumped up from his booth and lumbered toward the door. "I'll be right there."

Anger flared on Gandt's face as he spotted Dugan. "What the hell were you doing out at the Rankins ranch?"

Dugan squared his shoulders. "I just asked him some questions."

"That's my job." Sheriff Gandt poked Dugan in the belly. "Because of you nosing around, Wilbur Rankins just killed himself."

"What?"

"He shot himself, you bastard."

Dugan's mind raced. "Wilbur Rankins was dying of cancer. Why would he kill himself?" To end his pain?

"His son said he was upset about that news broadcast about Ron Lewis swindling folks in Cobra Creek. Said his daddy was too humiliated to live with people knowing he'd been foolish enough to lose his land."

Dugan silently cursed. The story hadn't revealed any names, though. "You going out there now?"

"Yeah, I'm meeting the M.E."

"I'll go with you."

"Hell, no," Gandt said. "You've done enough damage. You're the last person Junior Rankins wants to see."

Dugan held his tongue. But as Gandt strode from the diner, doubts set in. Had Rankins really killed himself?

Or had someone murdered him because he'd talked to Dugan? Because they thought Rankins knew more about Lewis's death than he'd told them?

SAGE CLEANED THE ROOM the couple had stayed in, needing to expend some energy before she tried to sleep.

That bloody whistle kept taunting her.

She stripped the bed, dusted the furniture and scrubbed the bathroom, then put fresh linens on the bed and carried the dirty sheets downstairs to the laundry room. Benji's room with the jungle theme and his stuffed animals and trains beckoned her. After she started the wash, she went back to his room and traced her finger lovingly over his bedding and the blanket he'd been so attached to.

She lay back on the bed and hugged it to her, then studied the ceiling where she'd glued stars that lit up in the dark. Benji had been fascinated with the night sky. She could still hear him singing, *Twinkle, twinkle, little star,* as he watched them glittering on his ceiling.

Did he dream about her, or did he have nightmares of that car crash? Had he felt safe with Ron or frightened?

A sob tore from her throat. Where was he, dammit?

She gave in to the tears for a few minutes, then cut herself off as she'd done the past two years.

She could not give up hope.

Taking a deep breath to calm herself, she tucked the bear beneath Benji's blanket, then whispered good-night. One day she would bring Benji back here and he'd know that she'd never forgotten him. That not a day had gone by that she hadn't thought of him, wanted to see him, loved him.

She turned off the light and closed the door, then walked to her room and slipped on her pajamas, latching on to the hope that the news report would trigger someone's memory, or a stranger would see Benji in a crowd or at school and call in.

Exhausted, she crawled into bed and turned off the lights. Dugan's face flashed behind her eyes, the memory of his comforting voice soothing. Dugan was working the case.

If anyone could find her son, he could.

Outside, the wind rattled the windowpanes, jarring her just as she was about to fall asleep. A noise sounded in the hall. Or was it downstairs?

She pushed the blanket away to go check, but suddenly the sound of someone breathing echoed in the room.

Fear seized her.

Someone was inside her bedroom.

She needed a weapon, but she didn't have a gun. If she could reach her phone…

She moved her hand to try to grab it off the nightstand, but suddenly the figure pounced on top of her, and a cold hard hand clamped down over her mouth.

"Lewis is dead. If you don't stop asking questions, you'll be next."

Chapter Eleven

A cold chill engulfed Sage.

"Did you do something to my son?" she whispered.

"Just let it go," he hissed against her ear.

The fear that seized Sage turned to anger. She would never let it go.

Determined to see the man's face, she shoved an elbow backward into his chest. He bellowed, slid his hands around her throat and squeezed her neck.

Sage tried to scream, but he pushed her face down into the pillow, crawled on top of her and jammed his knee into her back, using his weight to hold her down.

"I warned you."

Sage struggled against him and clawed at the bedding, but he squeezed her neck so hard that he was cutting off the oxygen. She gasped and fought, but she couldn't breathe, and the room spun into darkness.

DUGAN PLUGGED ALL the aliases Ron had used into the computer, then entered the name Janet to see if he could find a match.

The computer scrolled through all the names but didn't locate anyone named Janet associated with any of the aliases. The name Janelle popped, though.

Janelle Dougasville lived in a small town outside

Crystal City, one of the addresses listed for Mike Martin. Dugan checked records and discovered she had a rap sheet for petty crimes and was currently on parole for drug charges. He jotted down the address. He'd pay her a visit first thing in the morning.

If she'd been in contact with Lewis around the time he'd disappeared, she might have known his plans and the reason he'd taken Benji with him.

If he'd known he was in trouble, why take a child with him? A child that would slow him down and bring more heat down on him?

It didn't make sense.

What if he'd left Benji with someone before the accident? Was it possible he'd dropped him off with an accomplice? Maybe with Janelle?

His phone buzzed, and he checked the number. Not one he recognized, but he pressed Answer. It might be a tip about Benji. "Dugan Graystone."

"Mr. Graystone, this is D. J. Rankins."

Dugan frowned. "D.J.?"

"Wilbur's grandson. I saw you at the house before, when you came and talked to my dad."

"Right. I'm sorry to hear about your grandfather."

A labored breath rattled over the line. "That's why I'm calling. You came asking him about his land, and he was real upset. He and Daddy got in a big fight after you and that lady left."

What was the boy trying to tell him? "What happened?"

"Daddy called Grandpa an old fool for falling for that Lewis man's scheme, and Grandpa yelled at Daddy to get out, accused Daddy of waitin' on Grandpa to kick the bucket so he could get his land. Then Daddy grabbed his rifle and stalked off."

"Was that when your grandfather killed himself?"

A tense minute passed. Then Dugan thought he heard a sniffle.

"D.J.?"

"Yeah, I'm here. I...probably ought not to be callin'. My dad is gonna be real mad."

But still the kid had called. "D.J., you called because you thought it was the right thing to do. Now, tell me what's on your mind."

Another sniffle. "I don't think Grandpa killed himself."

Sage slowly roused back to consciousness. The room was dark, and she couldn't breathe. The musty odor of sweat and another smell...cigarette smoke? A cigar? Shoe polish?

Dizzy and disoriented, she rolled to her side and searched the room.

What had happened?

She gasped, her hand automatically going to her throat and rubbing her tender skin as the memory of the intruder surfaced. The man...big...heavy...on top of her, holding her down. Strangling her...

Those threatening words. "Lewis is dead. If you don't stop asking questions, you'll be next."

God... Was he still in the inn?

She froze, listening for his voice. His breathing?

But only the sound of the furnace rumbling echoed back.

The wind rattling the panes had woken her. He must have broken a window downstairs and snuck in.

Trembling, she slid from bed, grabbed the phone and punched Dugan's number. She hurried to look out the window, searching for her attacker outside, but clouds obscured the moon, painting the backyard a dismal gray.

The phone rang a second time as she hurried to her bedroom door and peered into the hallway. Downstairs seemed quiet, but what if he was still in the house?

The phone clicked. "Sage?"

"Dugan, someone broke into the inn. He...threatened me."

"Is he still there?"

"I don't think so," Sage said.

"Where are you?"

"In my bedroom."

"Lock yourself inside and don't come out. I'll call you when I arrive."

Sage stepped back inside the room, closed the door and locked it. She flipped on the light, then looked into the mirror above her vanity. Her hair looked wild, her eyes puffy, the imprint of a man's fingers embedded into her neck.

She tried to recall the details of her attack. How big her attacker was, how tall... Had she felt his beard stubble against her cheek when he'd whispered that threat in her ear?

Fear clouded her memory, but she heard his voice playing over and over in her head. A gruff, deep voice. Definitely male.

But who was he?

DUGAN SPED FROM his ranch toward Cobra Creek, his heart hammering. Sage had sounded shaken, but she was all right.

Unless the intruder was still there....

His tires squealed as he swerved down Main Street, then hung a right into the drive for the B and B. The drive was empty, but he spotted Sage's car in the detached garage. He scanned the street and property, searching for someone lurking around.

A dog roamed the street but took off running when his headlights startled him. A trash can lid rolled across the neighboring drive, clanging. Down the street, a truck rumbled, heading out of town.

Could it be the intruder's?

He hesitated, considered following it, but what if Sage's attacker was still in the house?

He flipped off his lights, parked and cut the engine. Pulling his weapon from the holster inside his jacket, he texted Sage that he was outside. Then he slowly approached the inn.

The front door was locked, and no one was around, so he eased his way to the fence, unlatched the gate and stepped inside, scanning the property. At least two miles of wooded land backed up to the creek. A walking trail wove through the woods, and park benches were situated by the water for guests to lounge and relax.

Sage didn't have enough land for horseback riding, but a ranch close by catered to guests craving the western experience. That ranch belonged to Helen Wiley, a middle-aged woman who loved kids and families and offered riding lessons to locals and tourists.

The silhouette of an animal combing the woods caught his eye, and he stepped nearer the woods to check it out. Deciding it was a deer, he turned and glanced at the back of the inn.

A rustic deck spanned the entire back side, with seating areas for guests to relax and enjoy the scenery. The deck was empty now, although one of the windows was open, a curtain flapping in the wind.

The intruder must have broken in through the window.

He kept his gun trained as he climbed the steps to the deck, then he checked the open window. The glass was broken. He'd come back and look for prints.

Right now he wanted to see Sage, make sure she was safe.

His phone buzzed with a text, and he glanced at it. Sage wanted to know where he was.

He texted, Back door.

He turned the doorknob and it opened easily. The intruder had obviously snuck in through the window but exited the back door, leaving it unlocked.

Didn't Sage have a damn alarm?

He inched inside the kitchen, tensing at the sound of footsteps on the stairs. Keeping his gun braced at the ready, he crept through the kitchen to the hallway and waited.

Seconds later, Sage came running down the stairs. Pale and terrified, she threw herself into his arms.

SAGE HAD BEEN alone with her grief and fears and the terrifying questions in her head for so long that she couldn't drag herself away from Dugan.

How long had it been since someone had held her? Taken care of her?

Two years…but any affection Ron had had for her had been an act.

Dugan stroked her back, soothing her. "It's okay now, Sage."

She nodded against him, but she couldn't stop trembling. "He choked me until I passed out."

His big body went so still that she felt the anxiety coiled in his muscles. "God, Sage."

He pulled away just enough to tilt her face up so he could examine her. Rage darkened his eyes when he spotted the bruises.

"Did you get a look at him?" Dugan asked, his voice low. Lethal.

She shook her head, her heart fluttering with awareness as he traced a finger along her throat. "It was too dark. And he threw me facedown on the bed and shoved my head into the pillows."

"What else do you remember?"

"He smelled like sweat and something else—maybe

cigarette smoke? He said Lewis was dead and that if I didn't stop asking questions, I'd be next."

"Damn," Dugan muttered.

Her gaze locked with his, the fierceness of a warrior in his eyes. Eyes the color of a Texas sunset.

Eyes full of dark emotion—anger, bitterness, maybe distrust.

And hunger. Hunger followed by a wariness that made her realize that he felt the sexual chemistry between them just as she did.

"Stay here. Let me search the rest of the inn."

She nodded and hugged the wall as he inched up the stairs to the second floor. His footsteps pounded above her as he moved from room to room. Seconds stretched into minutes, a moment of silence making her catch her breath in fear that her attacker had been hiding in one of the other rooms to ambush Dugan.

Finally, he appeared at the top of the staircase. "It's clear." He tucked his gun back into his holster and strode down the steps.

Sage's heart was beating so frantically that she reached for him.

Emotions clogged her throat as he tilted her chin up again.

But this time instead of examining her bruises, he closed his mouth over hers.

Sage gave in to the moment and savored the feel of his passion. She parted her lips in invitation, relishing the way he played his tongue along her mouth and growled low in his throat.

Hunger emanated from him, in the way his hands stroked her back, and the way his body hardened and melded against hers.

A warmth spread through her, sparking arousal and titillating sensations, earth-shattering in their intensity.

Dugan splayed his hands over her hips, drawing her closer, and she felt his thick erection press into her belly.

She wanted him.

Wanted to forget all the sadness and grief that had consumed her the past two years. Wanted to feel pleasure for a few brief moments before reality yanked her back to the ugly truth.

That her son was still missing.

Those very words made her pull away. What was wrong with her? Was she so weak that she'd fall into any man's arms?

She certainly had made that mistake with Ron.

She looked into Dugan's eyes and saw the same restless hunger that she felt. She also saw his turmoil.

He hadn't expected her to react like that to him.

It couldn't happen again.

DUGAN CURSED HIMSELF for his weakness. But one look into Sage's vulnerable eyes and he couldn't not kiss her.

Pain radiated from her in waves. For the first time, he'd forgotten about his resolve to keep his hands off her. She'd needed him.

And he'd needed to hold her and know that that bastard who'd tried to choke her hadn't succeeded.

Why had her attacker let her live? Did he really think he'd scare her so badly she'd stop looking for her son?

Chapter Twelve

Dugan adopted his professional mask, relieved she'd donned a robe over her long pajamas before he'd arrived. If he'd seen a sliver of her delicate skin, he might lose control, change his mind and take her to bed. "I'll check your room for prints."

"He wore gloves," Sage said. "Leather."

"Figures. Still, I'll look around in case he dropped something or left a stray hair."

She led the way, and he spent the next half hour searching her room. When he spotted the bed where she'd been sleeping when she was attacked, images of the man shoving her facedown assaulted him.

He was going to catch this jerk and made him suffer.

Sage excused herself to go to the bathroom while he searched the room. Grateful for the reprieve, he forced his mind on the task and checked the sheets. He ran his hands over the bedding but found nothing, so he stooped down to the floor and shone a small flashlight across the braided rug.

A piece of leather caught his attention. A strip, like part of a tassel to a boot or glove or jacket. Sage had said her attacker had worn gloves.

Hoping to find forensic evidence on it, he dragged on gloves and picked it up.

Sage emerged from the bathroom, her hair brushed, her robe cinched tight. "Did you find anything?"

He dangled the leather strip in front of her. "Do you recognize this?"

Sage shook her head no. "It's not mine."

"You struggled with the man?"

She shivered. "Yes."

"I'll bag this and send it to the lab." He strode toward the door. "Go back to bed, Sage. I'll stay downstairs and keep watch."

"I don't think I can sleep," Sage said, her voice as forlorn as the expression on her face.

Hell, he knew he wouldn't sleep. Not while worrying about Sage's attacker returning to make good on that threat.

And not while thinking about that damn kiss.

"Then just rest. I'm going to find something to fix that broken window."

She tugged at the top of her robe, pulling it together. "There's some plywood in the garage."

"That'll work." He forced his gaze away from her. "You need a security system."

"That's hard to do with guests."

"You can arrange a key system."

"Won't that be expensive?"

"It'll be worth it for you and your guests."

"I'll look into it," Sage agreed.

He turned to go down to the garage.

"Thank you for coming tonight, Dugan."

He paused, shoulders squared. "I'm going to catch this bastard and find Benji."

The soft whisper of her breath echoed between them. "I know you will."

Her confidence sent a warmth through him. Other than Jaxon, he'd never had anyone believe in him.

Especially a woman.

He didn't want to disappoint her.

Shaken by the thought, he rushed outside to the garage, found a toolbox and some plywood in the corner.

It took him less than ten minutes to cover the broken glass. When he'd finished, he walked around the other rooms, checking locks and windows and looking for other evidence the intruder might have left behind.

Then he made a pot of coffee and kept watch over the house until morning. But Sage's Christmas tree haunted him as the first strains of sunlight poured through the window.

More than anything, he wanted to bring Benji back to Sage for Christmas.

SAGE DIDN'T THINK she would sleep, but exhaustion, stress and worry had taken their toll, and she drifted off. She dreamed about Benji and the holidays and the attack. She felt the man's fingers closing around her neck, his knee jamming into her back, his weight on her. She was suffocating, couldn't breathe...

She jerked awake, disoriented for a moment. She scanned the room, searching the corners as reality returned. She was safe. The intruder was gone.

Knowing Dugan was downstairs watching out for her, she closed her eyes again. This time after she drifted off, she dreamed that Dugan was in bed with her, kissing her, stripping her clothes, making love to her...

When she stirred from sleep, her body felt achy and languid, content yet yearning for something more. More of Dugan's touches.

But sleeping with him would be a mistake. She wasn't the kind of woman who could crawl in bed with a man and walk away. She was too old-fashioned. Making love meant more to her than just a warm body.

Still, she craved his arms and hands on her.

Frustrated, she jumped in the shower. One blast of the cold water and she woke to reality. She adjusted the nozzle to warm and washed her hair, letting the soothing spray of water pulse against her skin until she felt calmer.

Finally she dried off, dressed and hurried down the stairs. Dugan had cooked eggs and bacon, and poured her a cup of coffee as soon as she entered. With remnants of the dream still playing through her head, the scene seemed cozy. Intimate.

What in the world was she thinking?

She and men didn't work.

"Last night before you called, I looked for Lewis's sister."

Sage blew on her coffee to cool it. "You found her?"

"I discovered a woman named Janelle Dougasville who lived near one of the addresses for Mike Martin."

"Have you talked to her?"

"Not yet. I'm planning to pay her a visit after breakfast."

"Then let's go."

"Eat something first."

"Dugan—"

He gestured toward the plate. "Humor me. I need food in the morning."

She agreed only because he made himself an egg sandwich using the toast he'd buttered, and wolfed it down. Her stomach growled, and she joined him at the table and devoured the meal.

"Thank you," she said. "I'm not accustomed to anyone cooking me breakfast. Usually that's my job."

Dugan shrugged. "Breakfast is the only meal I make."

She smiled, grateful for the small talk as they cleaned up the dishes.

"Where does this woman live?" Sage asked as they walked outside and settled in his SUV.

"Near Crystal City." He drove onto the main street. "I'll drop that leather strip at the lab on the way."

She glanced at the holiday decorations as they wove through town. Wreaths and bows adorned the storefronts. A special twelve-foot tree had been decorated and lit in the town square, and a life-size sleigh for families and children to pose for pictures sat at the entrance to the park where Santa visited twice a day.

Signs for a last-minute sale on toys covered the windows of the toy store. The bakery was running a special on fruit cakes and rum cakes, with no charge for shipping.

Soon Christmas would be here. Kids would be waking up to find the presents Santa had left under the tree. Families would be gathering to exchange gifts and share turkey and the trimmings.

The children's Christmas pageant at church was tonight.

Tears blurred her eyes. If Benji was here, they would go. But she couldn't bear it...not without him.

"I stopped by the diner for dinner after I left your place, and ran into Sheriff Gandt."

Thoughts of holiday celebrations and family vanished. "What did he have to say?"

"Wilbur Rankins killed himself last night after we left him."

Sage gasped. "Because of our questions?"

"His son claims he was ashamed over being swindled," Dugan said.

"Oh, my God." She twisted her hands together. "But the news story didn't name names."

"There's more," Dugan said. "D. J. Rankins, Wilbur's grandson, called me. He thinks his grandfather didn't commit suicide."

"What?"

"Apparently his father and grandfather argued after we left."

The implications in Dugan's voice disturbed her. "You think Junior Rankins killed his father?"

"I don't know," Dugan said. "But if he didn't, someone else might have."

Because they were asking questions. Because of the news story.

She'd been threatened, too.

Which meant she and Dugan were both in danger.

TWO HOURS LATER, Dugan parked at the address he found for Janelle Dougasville. The woman lived in a small older home, with neighboring houses in similar disrepair.

According to the information he'd accessed, she didn't have a job. A sedan that had once been red but had turned a rusted orange sat in the drive.

"If Ron had made money on other scams, he certainly didn't share it with the other women in his life."

"True. And if one of those women discovered he was lying about who he was, that he had other women, or that he was hoarding his money for himself, it would be motive for murder."

That meant Carol Sue Tinsley and Maude Handleman were both viable suspects. So was Beverly Vance.

Dugan knocked, his gaze perusing the property. The cookie-cutter houses had probably looked nice when new, but age and weather had dulled the siding, and the yards desperately needed landscaping.

Inside, the house was dark, making him wonder if Janelle was home. He knocked again, and seconds later, a light flickered on.

Beside him, Sage fidgeted.

The sound of the lock turning echoed and then the door opened. A short woman with dirty blond hair stared up at them, her nose wrinkled.

"Yeah?"

"Ms. Dougasville," Dugan said. "We'd like to talk to you."

The woman snorted. "You the law?"

"No." Dugan started to explain, but Sage spoke up.

"We're looking for my little boy. His name is Benji Freeport. You may have seen the news story about him. He disappeared two years ago."

The woman hunched inside her terry-cloth robe, her eyes squinting. "What's that got to do with me?"

"Probably nothing," Dugan said. "But if you'll let us in, we'll explain."

"Please," Sage said softly.

A second passed, then the woman waved them into the entryway. Dugan noted the scent of booze on her breath, confirmed by the near-empty bottle of whiskey sitting on the coffee table in the den.

Janelle gestured toward the sofa, and he and Sage took seats while she poured herself another drink. Her hand shook as she turned up the glass. "All right. What do you want?"

Dugan explained about Ron Lewis, his scams and phony identities.

"I don't understand why Ron took my little boy with him that day," Sage said, "but I've been looking for him ever since."

Janelle lit a cigarette, took a drag and blew smoke through her nose. "I don't know anything about your kid."

Sage sagged with disappointment.

"What can you tell us about Ron Lewis? He was your brother?" Dugan asked.

Janelle sipped her whiskey. "Not by birth. We grew up in the foster system together."

"Do you know his real name?"

She snorted. "I'm not sure he knows it."

"What was he called as a boy?"

"Lewis was his first name."

"So that's why he chose it this last time," Sage said. Had he planned to keep it? "Tell us more about his childhood."

"He was a quiet kid. His folks beat him till he was black-and-blue. First time I got put in the same foster with him, he told me they were dirt poor. He was half-starved, had one of them bloated bellies like you see on the kids on those commercials."

"Go on," Dugan said when she paused to take another drag on the cigarette.

"We was about the same age, you know. My story was just about like his, except I never had a daddy, just a whore for a mama. So we connected, you know."

"When was the last time you saw him?"

She tapped ashes into a soda can on the table. "About three years ago. He showed up one day out of the blue, said he was on to something big and that he was finally going to make all those things we dreamed about come true." A melancholy look softened the harsh lines fanning from her eyes. "When we got sent to the second foster home together, we made a pact that one day we'd get out and make something of ourselves."

Judging from her situation, Dugan doubted Janelle had succeeded.

"We used to go down to the creek and skip rocks and dream about being rich. I used to dream about us getting married and having a real family."

"Did Ron…I mean, Lewis, share that dream?" Sage asked.

Janelle shrugged. "He said he wanted all that, but he also lied a lot. Every time we got moved to a new foster, he took on the people's names."

That fit with his ability to assume different identities. He'd learned early on to switch names and lives.

Dugan would have felt sorry for him if he hadn't destroyed lives and hurt Sage so much.

"Tell me more about his real parents," Sage said.

"His daddy blew all he made on the races, and his mama liked meth."

"Do you know what happened to them?"

"Last we talked, he said his mama died. Don't know about his old man. Seems like I heard he got killed, probably by one of the bookies he owed money to."

Sage sighed, a frustrated sound. "Was there anyone else he might go to if he was in trouble? Another girlfriend?"

Janelle stubbed out her cigarette and tossed down the rest of her whiskey. "There was one girl he had a thing for bad. A real thing, I mean, like he wasn't just using her. He was young when it happened, but they talked about getting married."

"What was her name?"

"Sandra Peyton," Janelle said bitterly. "He knocked her up, but she lost the baby, and things fell apart."

Dugan made a mental note of the woman's name. If Sandra was the love of Lewis's life and he thought he'd finally made the fortune he wanted, maybe he had been going to see her, to win her back again.

Another thought nagged at Dugan—what if he was taking Benji to replace the child they'd lost?

Chapter Thirteen

Dugan stopped for lunch at a barbecue place called The Pig Pit, but Sage's appetite had vanished. She kept replaying the story Janelle Dougasville had told her about Ron Lewis...rather Lewis, the foster kid.

His upbringing had definitely affected him, had motivated him to want more from life, especially material things. He was trying to make up for what he hadn't had as a child.

Being shuffled from one foster family to another had turned him into a chameleon. A man who could deftly switch names, lives and stories with no qualms or hesitation.

A man who had learned to manipulate people to get what he wanted.

One who played the part but remained detached, because getting attached to a family or person was painful when you were forced to leave that family or person behind.

That, Dugan could relate to.

"I almost feel sorry for him," Sage said, thinking out loud.

"Don't." Dugan finished his barbecue sandwich. "Sure, he had some hard knocks in life, but a lot of people have crappy childhoods and don't turn out to be liars and con artists."

"You're right. He could just as easily have turned that trauma into motivation for really making something of himself."

"You mean something respectful," Dugan clarified. "Because he was something. A liar and a master manipulator."

"Yes, he was." Sage sighed. "If he really loved this woman, Sandra Peyton, do you think he might have tried to reconnect with her?"

"Anything is possible."

Sage contemplated that scenario. If Sandra Peyton had Benji, at least she was probably taking care of him and he was safe.

But where was she?

DUGAN SNATCHED HIS PHONE and punched in a number as they left the restaurant and got in the car. "Jaxon, it's Dugan. Did you learn anything about that women's shelter where Carol Sue volunteered?"

"Women there are hush-hush," Jaxon said. "But when I explained that Benji might have been kidnapped they were cooperative. That said, no one saw him, and the lady who runs the house denied that Carol Sue brought Benji there."

A dead end.

"See if you can locate a woman named Sandra Peyton."

"Who is she?"

"Lewis's foster sister, Janelle Dougasville, claims that he was involved with Sandra Peyton years ago, so he might have reconnected with her."

"I'm on it."

Dugan's other line was buzzing, so he thanked Jaxon and answered the call. "Graystone."

"Mr. Graystone, this is Ashlynn Fontaine. I ran the story

for Ms. Freeport about her son in the paper, and my friend covered it on the news."

"Yes."

"Ms. Freeport gave me your number to contact in case any leads came in regarding her son."

His pulse spiked. "You have something?"

"I received a call from an anonymous source who said that a woman and a little boy Benji's age moved in next to her about a month after Ms. Freeport's son went missing. She's not certain the child is Benji, but she said the woman was very secretive and kept to herself. Thought you might want to check it out."

"Text me her name and address."

A second later, the text came through. Dugan headed toward the address. It might be a false lead.

Then again, maybe they'd get lucky and this child might be Sage's missing son.

SAGE CLENCHED HER HANDS together as Dugan explained about the call.

"I hope this pans out, Sage," Dugan said. "But normally when a tip line is set up, it triggers a lot of false leads."

Sage nodded. She knew he was trying to prepare her for the possibility that this child might not be her son, but still, a seed of hope sprouted. Even if it wasn't Benji, maybe the tip line would work and someone would spot him.

Worry mounted inside her, though, as he drove. The half hour drive felt like years, and by the time they arrived, she'd twisted the locket around her neck a hundred times. Her neck still felt sore from the attack, the bruises darkening to an ugly purple.

A stark reminder that someone wanted her dead.

The woman lived in a small ranch-style house with a giant blow-up Santa Claus in front and a Christmas tree with blinking, colored lights visible through the front window.

Sage's heart squeezed. If Benji was here, at least the woman was taking care of him and decorated for the holidays.

Although resentment followed. Those precious moments had been stolen from her.

Dugan parked on the curb a few feet down from the house. The front door opened and a woman wearing a black coat stepped out, one hand clutching a leash attached to a black Lab, the other hand holding a small child's.

Sage pressed her face against the glass to see the boy more clearly, but he wore a hooded navy jacket. He looked about five, which was the correct age, but she couldn't see his eyes.

Sorrow and fear clogged Sage's throat. Children changed in appearance every day. What if Benji had changed so much she didn't recognize him?

Sage started to reach for the door to get out of the SUV, but he laid his hand over hers. "Wait. Let's just watch for a few minutes. We don't want to spook her."

As much as Sage wanted to run to the boy, Dugan was right. If this woman had her son and knew Sage was searching for them, she might run.

Dugan pulled a pair of binoculars from beneath his seat and handed them to her, then retrieved a camera from the back, adjusted the lens and snapped some photographs. She peered through the binoculars, focusing on the little boy and the woman.

The woman kept a tight hold on the child's hand. A natural, protective gesture? Or was she afraid he might try to get away?

Stories of other kidnappings where the victims identified with their kidnapper nagged at her. Benji had been only three when he was abducted.

Did he even remember her?

Or had he bonded with whoever had'him? If it was a woman, did he think she was his mother?

A pang shot through her. Did he call her Mom?

DUGAN SENSED THE TENSION radiating from Sage. Hell, he couldn't blame her. She hadn't seen her son in two years—she was probably wondering what he looked like now. If he would even recognize her.

If he was alive and had been living with another woman or a family, he might have developed Stockholm syndrome.

He studied the body language of the woman and child as she spoke to the little boy. They seemed completely at ease with each other. The boy was saying something, and she tilted her head toward him with a smile. They swung hands as they rounded the corner, then paused while the dog sniffed the grass in a neighboring yard.

"I can't really see his face," Sage said.

"I don't have a good shot of it, either," Dugan admitted. "When they reach the house, and he takes his coat off, maybe we'll get a better look."

The dog nuzzled up to the little boy, and the kid laughed. Then the woman looked up and scanned the streets, as if nervous. A second later, he swore her gaze latched with his.

Dugan lowered the camera to the seat. "I think she spotted us," Dugan said. "Drop the binoculars, Sage."

Dugan pulled a map from the side pocket of the car and pretended he was looking at it. But he continued to watch the woman and boy out of the corner of his eye.

"He looks happy and well taken care of," Sage said in a voice laced with a mixture of pain and relief.

Dugan gave her a sympathetic look. The woman suddenly turned and ushered the boy and dog back toward the house. This time, instead of walking leisurely, she picked up her pace and looked harried. Even frightened.

Sage sat up straighter. "She looks scared. Maybe we should go talk to her."

Dugan shook his head. "Wait. Let's watch and see what she does."

Sage's frustrated sigh echoed through the SUV. "What if she runs?"

"Then we'll follow her."

Panic streaked Sage's voice. "But if it's Benji, I don't want to lose him again."

Dugan wanted to promise her she wouldn't, but he bit back the words. They didn't know for certain that this was Benji.

When the woman reached the walkway to her house, she broke into a jog, half dragging the dog and the boy. She ushered them both inside, then shut the door.

But not before glancing over at them again. Fear had flashed in her eyes.

Dugan's pulse pounded.

What was she running from?

SAGE DUG HER FINGERNAILS into her palms to keep from opening the SUV door and bolting toward the house. She desperately wanted to see the little boy's face.

And the woman was definitely afraid.

Memories of Benji smiling up at her as a baby with his gap-toothed grin taunted her. His curly blond hair, the light in his green eyes, his chubby baby cheeks... Then he'd turned from a pudgy toddler to a three-year-old overnight.

More memories flooded her—his first words, the way he loved blueberries and called them BBs, his attachment to a pair of cartoon pajamas and the yellow rubber boots he'd worn to play in the rain.

The side door to the house opened, and the boy and dog spilled out. The dog barked and raced across the fenced-in yard, and the boy ran over to the swing set and climbed the jungle gym. She needed to see his ear, that piece of cartilage....

The hood to his jacket slipped down, and she stared at the mop of blond hair. Her breath caught, lungs straining for air.

Could it be her son?

Suddenly a siren wailed, and Dugan cursed. She looked over her shoulder and spotted the sheriff's car rolling up behind them.

"Damn. She must have called the law," Dugan said.

Sage bit her tongue. Would she have done that if she was hiding out with a child that the police were searching for?

Dugan shoved the camera to the floor, and she slid the binoculars into her purse. The sheriff's car door slammed, and then he hitched up his pants and strode toward them, a sour look pinching his face.

He tapped on the driver's window, and Dugan powered the window down. "Sheriff," Dugan muttered.

Sheriff Gandt leaned forward, pinning her and Dugan with his scowl. "What are you two doing here?"

Dugan indicated the map. "Just stopped, looking for directions."

"Don't lie to me," Sheriff Gandt growled. "Get out of the car."

Sage clenched the door handle. Was he going to arrest them?

Dugan opened the door, climbed out and leaned against the side of the SUV. She walked around the front of the vehicle and joined him.

Sheriff Gandt hooked a thumb toward the house. "The woman that lives inside there called, freaked out, said a couple was stalking her and her child."

Sage's stomach knotted. "We weren't stalking them."

"But you were watching them," Sheriff Gandt said, one bushy eyebrow raised.

Dugan cleared his throat. "We had a tip we were following up on."

"What kind of tip?"

"From the news story that aired about Benji," Sage explained. "Someone called with suspicions that the woman who lives here might have Benji."

Sheriff Gandt mumbled an ugly word. "Then you should have called me."

Why would she call him when he hadn't helped her before? When she didn't trust him?

DUGAN BARELY RESISTED slugging the imbecile. He should be following up on leads, searching for Benji, but so far he'd either been incompetent or just didn't care. "We assumed you were busy investigating Rankins's supposed suicide."

Gandt's eyebrows crinkled together. "What the hell does that mean?"

"Are you sure it was a suicide?" Dugan asked.

"Of course it was. His own son called me. Said he heard his daddy pull the trigger."

"Did you check Junior for gunshot residue?" Dugan asked.

Anger reddened Sheriff Gandt's cheeks. "Wasn't no need. His daddy was upset about your visit and he was dying of cancer and decided to end his misery. End of story." Gandt planted his fists on his hips. "Besides, I'm not the one breaking the law here. You are."

"We didn't break the law," Sage said.

"You scared that poor woman to death," Gandt said. "She thought you were child predators, here to steal her son."

Sage stiffened. Those words hit too close to home. "Maybe she's afraid because she's the one who stole Benji, and now that the story aired about him again, she's terrified someone will recognize Benji and call the police."

Which was exactly what had happened.

Gandt looked exasperated, but Dugan didn't intend to let him off the hook. If the kid inside was Benji, once they left, the woman would take him and run.

Then they might never find him again.

"There's one way we can settle this," Dugan said. "Let's go talk to her."

Sheriff Gandt huffed. "That could be considered harassment."

"Then go with us," Sage suggested. "You can explain the circumstances. If she has nothing to hide, she'll talk to us. And if that little boy isn't Benji, then we'll go on our way and she won't ever see or hear from us again."

Gandt looked annoyed and frustrated, but he heaved a weary breath. "All right. But if she insists on pressing charges against you, I won't stop her."

Dugan nodded and pressed his hand to the small of Sage's back as they followed the sheriff up to the door.

He could feel Sage trembling beneath his touch as Gandt rang the doorbell.

Chapter Fourteen

Sage held her breath as they waited on the woman inside to open the door.

When she did, her wary look made Sage's heart pound.

"Ms. Walton," Sheriff Gandt said. "I came as soon as I got your call."

Dark hair framed an angular face that might have been pretty had it not been for the severe scowl pulling at her mouth and the jagged scar that ran down her left cheek. A scar Sage hadn't noticed from a distance because of the coat and scarf the woman had been wearing.

Ms. Walton glanced back and forth between Sage and Dugan, her eyes angry. "Why were you two watching me?"

"Can we please come in and explain?" Sage said, grateful her voice didn't quiver and betray her.

Ms. Walton looked at the sheriff, who rolled his shoulders. "They're not stalkers," he said, although his tone indicated they were barely a notch above it.

"I'm a private investigator," Dugan said. "And this woman is Sage Freeport. You may have seen the recent news story that aired about her missing son, Benji Freeport."

The woman clenched the door in a death grip as if she was ready to slam it in their faces and flee. "I don't see what that has to do with me."

"Maybe nothing," Sage said. "But we received an anonymous tip that you might know something about my little boy."

"Me?" Shock strained the woman's voice. "I don't know anything." She angled her head toward the sheriff. "Now, are you going to make them leave me alone?"

"Yes, ma'am, I'm sorry—"

"We're not leaving until you answer some questions," Dugan said.

Gandt shot him a warning look.

"I told you I don't know anything about your little boy, Ms. Freeport. But I am sorry about what happened to you, and I hope you find him."

Sage swallowed hard. The woman sounded sincere.

But if she was innocent, why was she so nervous?

DUGAN STUDIED MS. WALTON's body language. She was definitely scared and hiding something.

But what?

"Did you know a man named Ron Lewis?"

"No." A noise sounded behind them, and Dugan realized it was the back door shutting. The little boy was coming back inside.

"How about Mike Martin or Seth Handleman or Joel Bremmer?"

"No, who are those people?"

"Aliases of Ron Lewis, the man who abducted Benji Freeport."

"I told you, I don't know any of them." She started to shut the door, but Sage caught it this time.

"How old is your little boy?" Sage asked.

A dark look crossed the woman's face. "He'll be six next week."

Sage's sigh fluttered in the tension-laden air. "What's his name?"

Ms. Walton's eyes widened with alarm, as if she realized the implications of Sage's question. A second later, anger sparked. "I named him Barry after my father." Her tone grew sharp. "He is not your son, Ms. Freeport."

"Then, you have his birth certificate?" Dugan asked.

Panic flared in her expression. "I don't have to prove anything to you."

Sheriff Gandt made a low sound in his throat. "No, you don't, Ms. Walton." Sage opened her mouth to argue, but Gandt continued. "But if you have it, please get it and we'll clear this matter up. Then these folks will be on their way and I'll make sure they never bother you again."

"I...actually I don't have it here," she said shrilly. "It's in a safe-deposit box at the bank."

Dugan cleared his throat. "Then you won't mind bringing the boy to the door so we can meet him." Not that they still wouldn't need DNA if Sage recognized the child.

The fear that had earlier pervaded Ms. Walton's eyes deepened, but she looked directly at Sage. "He's not your son. He's mine."

Dugan gritted his teeth. Was that her way of telling Sage the truth? Or could she be mentally and emotionally unstable?

If she'd wanted a child and had lost one or hadn't been able to have a baby, she might have taken Benji and now perceived him as her own.

SAGE FORCED HERSELF not to react to Ms. Walton's possessive, defensive tone. Was she defensive because she was an honest, loving mother who had to defend herself?

Or because she was a kidnapper, afraid of getting caught?

"Just introduce us to the little boy," Dugan said.

Ms. Walton glanced at the sheriff, who managed a grunt. "Do it, ma'am. Then we'll be out of your hair."

Ms. Walton shot Sage a wary look. But she turned and yelled for Barry to come to her. A minute later, the child ran to the front door and slipped up beside his mother.

Sage soaked in his features. The wavy blond hair. The cherub face. The wide eyes that looked distrustful and full of fear.

Eyes that were brown, not green like her son's. And his ears…no extra piece of cartilage.

Disappointment engulfed her, and she released a pained breath. Dugan had warned her about getting up her hopes, but still she had latched on to the possibility.

He looked at her for a response, and Sage shook her head. She'd feared she wouldn't recognize her son, but she immediately knew that this precious little boy was not hers.

"Hi, Barry," Dugan said. "We saw you walking your dog. He's pretty cool."

Sage tried to speak, but her voice refused to come out.

"Well?" Sheriff Gandt said bluntly.

"No," Sage finally managed to say.

"I'm sorry we bothered you," Dugan said.

Relief softened the harsh lines of Ms. Walton's face, and she stooped down and kissed Barry. "Honey, why don't you get the spaghetti out of the pantry and we'll start dinner?"

Barry nodded eagerly and raced to the pantry. Ms. Walton squared her shoulders. "I'm sorry for you, Ms. Freeport. I didn't mean to overreact."

"But you were afraid," Sage said, still confused.

"I was. I am…" Her voice cracked. "My husband was abusive. He did this." She rubbed the scar along her cheek. "I had him arrested, but he keeps getting out of jail and looking for us. Barry and I went into a program and changed our names so he wouldn't find us."

"Why didn't you just tell us that when we first arrived?"

"I…when I saw you watching me, I was afraid he'd hired you to find us."

"You have a restraining order against him?" Sheriff Gandt asked.

"Yes," she said in a low voice, "but that didn't stop him before."

That explained the reason the caller said the woman stayed to herself and seemed nervous.

"I'm sorry," Sage said. "We honestly didn't mean to frighten you or your son." She reached inside her purse and handed the woman a card with her name and number. "I own the B and B in Cobra Creek. If you ever need anything, even just a friend to talk to, I'm there."

"I haven't made many friends 'cause I've been on the run. Thanks." Tears blurred the other woman's eyes as she gripped the card between her fingers. "I'll pray that you find your son."

Sage battled tears of her own. Tears for the woman whose little boy had to be afraid of his own father.

Tears for her child, who could be safe somewhere—or in danger from whomever had stolen him.

COMPASSION FOR SAGE filled Dugan as they walked back to his SUV. Gandt escorted them, his disapproval evident.

"You two need to go home and let me do my job. You can't be scaring women and children like this."

"We didn't mean to frighten them," Sage said.

Gandt's nostrils flared. "But you did."

"Only because she had something to hide," Dugan said, refusing to let Gandt intimidate him. If the man had done his job as he should have, Dugan wouldn't have jumped in to help Sage.

Gandt folded his beefy arms. "Hear me and hear me good. If I receive another call like this one, I'll lock both of you up just to get you off the street so that I *can* do my job."

With a deep grunt, he turned and strode back to his car. Dugan slid behind the steering wheel, irritated that

Gandt waited until Sage climbed in his SUV and he pulled away from the curb before he started his squad car.

The sound of Sage's breathing rattled between them.

He turned onto the main road, then sped back toward Cobra Creek, but his mind kept replaying that phone call from Junior Rankins's son.

Had Rankins killed himself because of the cancer or because he was embarrassed that he'd been duped by Lewis?

Or had someone killed Rankins because he'd talked to them? Because they feared he knew something that would lead them to Lewis's killer?

SAGE STRUGGLED TO hold herself together. If she fell apart, Dugan might drop her case.

But Benji's innocent face flashed in her mind, and she closed her eyes, vying for courage. A mother was supposed to protect her child. Keep him safe and guide him through life. Comfort him when he was scared, chase the monsters away and sacrifice everything to give him a good life.

She had failed at all of those.

She wrapped her arms around her middle, counting the minutes until they reached the B and B. Anxious to be alone and vent her emotions, she opened the SUV door as soon as Dugan parked.

The Christmas lights mocked her, twinkling along the street and the fence in front of the B and B. A blow-up Santa waved to her from across the street at the children's clothing shop, making her throat thick with unshed tears.

She wrestled with her keys, fumbling, then dropping them on the front porch. Dugan's footsteps pounded behind her. Then suddenly he was there, retrieving her keys and unlocking the door for her.

He caught her arm before she could rush inside. "Let me check the inn first."

God... She'd forgotten about the break-in and the attack.

He gestured for her to wait on the porch swing, and she sank onto it and knotted her hands together, looking out at the twinkling Christmas lights and the darkness as he pulled his gun and inched inside.

It felt like hours but was probably only minutes before he returned, holstering his gun as he approached. "It's clear."

She nodded, too upset to speak. If she lost it, he'd probably stop helping her and then she'd be all alone again, with no one looking for her son.

DUGAN KNEW HE should walk away. Leave Sage to deal with the fallout of the day.

Focus on the case.

He wanted to see the original file on the investigation into Benji's disappearance and Lewis's automobile accident.

But he'd made an enemy of Gandt, and the sheriff probably wouldn't hand over the file. So how could he get it?

Maybe the deputy? If he refused, he'd sneak in and steal it....

Sage looked up at him, her eyes luminous with unshed tears, then she stood and stepped toward the door.

"Thanks, Dugan."

Dammit, she was trying to be so strong. Holding herself together when he knew she was hurting inside.

He'd be a damn, cold-hearted bastard to walk away right now.

"I'm going to review the notes in the original file when Benji first disappeared," he said in a feeble attempt to soothe her.

She nodded, her back to him, clenching her purse strap with a white-knuckled grip. "You're not giving up?"

"No."

Hell, he wished he could. But he wanted answers now himself. Not just for her.

But for that innocent little boy out there who might be suffering God knows what. Who might not even know that his amazing mother missed him every day.

A mother who would sacrifice anything for her son.

Sage was strong and gutsy and tenderhearted and beautiful, both inside and out.

He stepped inside with her, so close he inhaled her scent. Some kind of floral fragrance that smelled natural, like a spring garden before the Texas summer heat robbed it of life.

She shivered, totally unaware of the effect she had on him.

Needing to touch her and reassure her that she wasn't alone, he rubbed her arms with his hands. "I made you a promise, and I intend to keep it. I won't stop until we know what happened to your son."

Sage turned toward him then, her face so angelic and tortured that it broke his heart. "No one keeps promises anymore," she whispered.

Dugan had let people down before. Hell, he'd let himself down.

But he would not let down this strong, loving woman who needed someone on her side.

"I do," he said simply.

But there was nothing simple about it. He just couldn't walk away.

Her gaze met his, and his heart clenched. A second later, he pulled her into his arms and kissed her, his lips telling her all the things that his heart couldn't say.

Chapter Fifteen

Sage felt as if she was unraveling from the inside out.

Dugan's arms around her gave her strength, and she leaned into him, grateful not to be alone.

His kiss set her on fire and aroused long-forgotten needs. Desperate for more, to be even closer to him, she parted her lips in invitation. Dugan made a low sound in his throat, a passionate sound that made her heart flutter.

He deepened the kiss, teasing her with his tongue as his hands raked down her back. Her nipples budded to hard peaks, aching for attention, and she threaded her fingers in his hair and moaned.

Titillating sensations tingled through her as he splayed his hands across her hips and pulled her closer. His thick length rubbed against her belly, stirring her passion.

He ended the kiss, then trailed his lips down her neck and teased the sensitive skin behind her ear. She moaned softly and unfastened the top button of his shirt. He lowered his head, his tongue dancing down her neck, and then he used his teeth to tug at the neckline of her sweater.

Sage wanted more.

She made quick work of his buttons, then pushed his shirt aside and kissed his neck and chest. His chest was rock solid, bronzed, muscles corded and hard. She traced his nipple with her tongue, then sucked it gently.

Dugan groaned, gripped her arms and pulled away. "We should stop."

"No," Sage said. "Please, Dugan. I don't want to be alone right now."

"And I don't want to take advantage of you," he said gruffly.

"You aren't." She raised her head and brushed her lips across his neck, a seductive maneuver that seemed to trigger his passion, then led him to her bedroom.

With a low groan, he tugged her sweater over her head. She lifted her arms, eager to be closer, for skin to touch skin. She pushed his shirt off and dropped it to the floor.

His dark gaze devoured her, his look hungry and appreciative. He gently eased her bra strap over her shoulder, then the other, and heat curled in her abdomen.

"You are beautiful," he said in a low, husky murmur.

Sage started to shake her head no. She didn't want words, didn't know if she believed them.

She simply wanted to feel tonight. To forget that he was with her only because she'd asked him to help her find Benji.

God…Benji…what was she doing?

Dugan must have realized her train of thought, because he tilted her chin up, forcing her to look into his eyes. The heat and hunger burning there sparked her own raw need.

"It's okay to feel, to take comfort," he said. "That doesn't mean you've forgotten your son. That you're a bad mother for needing someone."

Tears threatened, but his forgiving words soothed her nerves. The past two years, she had experienced guilt on a daily basis. Guilt for being alive when her little boy might not be.

"Shh, don't think," Dugan murmured against her ear.

She nodded and shut out the turmoil raging inside her as he kissed her again. He brushed his fingers across her nipples, teasing them again to stiff peaks, then he lowered his mouth and closed his lips over one nipple, sucking her gently and stirring sensations in her womb.

Sage reached for his belt buckle, her body burning with the need to have him inside her.

DUGAN CALLED HIMSELF all kinds of fool for letting things go as far as they had with Sage. But she'd looked too forlorn, defeated and disappointed for him to leave her alone tonight.

Her fingers skated over his chest, eliciting white-hot heat on his skin. Touched and honored that she wanted to be with him, he paused for a moment to drink in her beauty. Her breasts were high, round, firm.

One touch of his lips to her nipples and she clutched at him with a groan. He tugged the turgid peak between his teeth and suckled her, his own body on fire, with hunger for more.

The hiss of his zipper rasping on his jeans as she lowered it sounded erotic, and made him reach for hers, as well. He peeled them down her legs. A pair of the sheerest black lacy panties he'd ever seen accentuated her curves and hinted at the secrets that lay below.

His mouth watered.

She blushed at his perusal, and he threaded one hand into her hair while he trailed kisses along her neck and throat. She moaned and ran her hands down his chest, then over his hips, and his body jerked as sensations splintered through him.

She shoved his boxers down his thighs, and his sex sprang free, pulsing with need. Full, hard, thick. Then her hand closed around him, and he hissed between his teeth at the pure pleasure rippling through him.

But he had to slow things down. Tonight wasn't about him but about pleasing her. Giving her comfort. Reassuring her that it was okay for her to feel alive when she still had questions about her son.

Sometimes you had to feel that life in order to move past the darkness and survive.

He gently eased her down on the bed, his gaze raking in her feminine curves. She arched her back, like a contented cat, and he smiled, then tugged her lacy panties down over her hips. Cool air hardened her nipples again, making heat flood him as he rose above her and kissed her again.

Their tongues danced, mated, played a game of seduction, then he ripped his mouth from hers and trailed his tongue down her body again. He made love to her with his mouth, suckling each breast until she threw back her head and groaned. Then his tongue played down her torso, circled her belly button, and dipped lower to taste her sweet essence.

He eased her legs farther apart, lifted her hips and drove his mouth over her heat, tasting, teasing, devouring her as a starving man would his last meal.

Seconds later, her release trembled through her. He savored her sweetness as she cried out his name and gave herself to him.

SAGE SHIVERED WITH mindless pleasure. She closed her eyes, clawing at the covers as sensation after sensation rippled through her.

Dugan didn't pull away, though, as Ron had done. He consumed her with his mouth.

She groaned his name and reached for him, wanting more. Needing more.

Craving all of him.

The muscles in his arms bunched and flexed as he finally rose above her. He had an athlete's muscular body, broad shoulders, corded muscles. And hints of his Native American heritage in his slick dark chest.

The fierceness of a warrior in his dark, endlessly sexy, bedroom eyes touched her soul.

Eyes that had once seemed distant and unbending but now flickered with stark, raw passion.

She lowered her hand, cradled his thick length in her palm and stroked him. He threw back his head on a guttural moan, and feminine power raged through her.

"I want you, Sage," he said between clenched teeth.

She stroked him again, guiding him to her core. "I want you, too."

His breath rattled in the air as he left her for a moment, and she twisted, achy and missing him. He dug a condom from the pocket of his jeans on the floor, and started to roll it on.

She held out her hand and urged him to come to her. His eyes flared with unadulterated lust as she slipped the condom over his erection.

With one quick thrust, he entered her. Sage's body exploded with need and pleasure. He pulled out and thrust back inside her again, filling her to the depths of her soul with his rawness.

She gripped his hips, angling hers so he could reach deeper, and he rasped her name, his movements growing faster and harder as he plunged inside her. She wrapped her legs around his waist and clutched his back, their skin gliding together as they built a frantic rhythm and another orgasm began to spike.

A deep animal-like sound erupted from his throat, his release triggering her own, and together they rode the waves of pleasure.

Dugan's labored breathing echoed in the air as they lay entwined in the aftermath of their lovemaking. But he pulled away too quickly and strode to her bathroom.

A minute later, he returned. His expression looked troubled, his body tense.

Naked, he was so sexy and masculine that she reached for him again. The familiar guilt threatened, but she shut it out and pulled him back in bed with her.

He wrapped his arms around her, and she curled against him. "Sage?"

"Don't say anything," she said softly. She especially didn't want an apology or promises that he couldn't keep.

She trusted him to help her find her son, but she'd vowed never to chance losing her heart again.

All she wanted tonight was to have him comfort her and keep her warm and chase away the nightmares.

Those would be waiting in the morning, just as they had been for the past two years.

DUGAN WAITED UNTIL Sage fell asleep, then slid from beneath the covers and dressed. He walked downstairs and outside to the back deck overlooking the creek.

Dammit, he shouldn't have taken Sage to bed.

Normally he considered himself a love-'em-and-leave-'em kind of guy. Sex was sex. No attachments. No emotional ties.

He was not the kind of man to stick around or to belong to a family. Hell, he'd never been part of a real one and figured he'd screw it up just as his old man had.

The old man he'd never known.

Besides, letting emotions get in the way caused him to lose focus. And right now he needed to focus on finding Benji.

That one lead hadn't panned out, but the little boy's picture was all over the news, so hopefully if he was still alive, someone would spot him.

Yeah, right. If whoever had Benji had kept his identity a secret for two years, they certainly wouldn't want to be found now. Worse, the story might cause the person to panic and flee the state, even the country.

To take on another name, go into hiding somewhere completely off the grid.

He texted Jaxon and asked him to be sure to alert airports, train stations, bus stations and border patrols to look for Benji.

Somewhere in the woods, leaves rustled. The wind whipped them into a frenzy. An animal howled.

He stepped closer to the end of the porch, searching the darkness. Was that a shadow near the creek?

Senses on alert, he studied the trees and creek edge, hunting for a predator.

Another noise, and he spotted a figure slipping behind a boulder.

Dugan pulled his gun from his holster, descended the porch steps and crept through the woods. The figure moved again, tree branches crackling. Something darted across the dark...the figure running?

He hunkered low, using the trees as cover as he moved closer. A noise to the right startled him, and he glanced toward it. A flicker of a light. A thin stream of smoke.

Hadn't Sage mentioned that her attacker smelled like cigarette smoke?

Had he returned to make good on his threat?

"THEY'VE GOT HALF the country looking for that little boy. You have to do something. No one can ever know what we did."

"Dammit, I'm doing the best I can."

"Kill the woman if you have to. She's getting too close. She went to see Janelle Dougasville today."

"What did that woman tell them?"

"She told them about Sandra Peyton."

Hell. The Dougasville woman should have kept her trap shut.

Now Sandra Peyton had to die.

Chapter Sixteen

Dugan rounded the corner of the oak, his gun drawn. "Hold it or I'll shoot."

A shriek echoed in the air, and then the silhouette of a man filled his vision. A thin young man with his hands up in surrender. "Please, don't shoot, mister."

Dugan frowned, then pulled a penlight from his pocket and aimed it at the guy. Damn. He was a teenager. A big guy who looked as though he might play football.

And he was shielding the girl behind him, who was frantically rebuttoning her blouse.

"A little cold to be out here in the woods this time of night, don't you think?" Dugan asked.

The boy shrugged, his leather jacket straining his linebacker shoulders. "We weren't doing anything wrong."

The girl yanked on a jacket, then inched up behind the guy, her eyes wide with fear. "Please don't hurt us, mister."

"I'm not here to hurt anyone," Dugan said, irritated they'd drawn him away from Sage's. What if someone really was watching her house, and Dugan was chasing two randy teenagers and that person got to Sage?

"I thought you were stalking the inn, here to cause trouble for the owner."

The boy said a dirty word that Dugan didn't even use

himself. "We came here 'cause Joy's mama won't let me come to the house."

"I can't say as I blame her," Dugan said, "considering you're mauling her daughter and cussing like a sailor."

"He wasn't mauling me," the girl said, her tone stronger now. "I'm seventeen. I make my own choices."

These teenagers weren't his problem. When he was the boy's age, he was probably doing the same thing.

Dugan tucked his gun back in his holster, then gestured for them to settle down. "Go on, get out of here." He gave the boy a warning look. "And don't come back to these woods again."

"No, sir, we won't." The boy grabbed the girl's hand, and they hurried back toward the wide part of the creek where they'd crossed in a small boat from the other side.

Something about seeing that boat nagged at Dugan. The creek ran wide and deep in certain areas and eventually emptied into the river that kayakers, rafters and boaters frequented. People could park in one area and boat to the other. In fact, rafters or boaters often parked cars in two areas, one where they put in and the other where they got out.

He remembered glancing at the report showing the location of Lewis's crash.

He wanted to see that report again. And he wanted to go back and walk the search grid, as well. Maybe the sheriff and his team had missed something.

The next morning Sage rolled over, sated and more rested than she had been in ages.

Memories of making love with Dugan the night before floated back in a euphoric haze.

But the bed beside her was empty. Not just empty but cold, as if Dugan hadn't slept there.

She'd been so deep in slumber that she hadn't even known when he'd left her bed.

Two years of exhausting, sleepless nights had finally caught up with her.

But morning sunlight poured through the window, slanting rays of light across the wood floors and reminding her that today was one more in a long list where Benji wasn't home.

One more day closer to another Christmas she would spend alone.

God, she was so tired of being alone.

Her heart clenched as if in a vise. What if she never found him? Could she go on day after day without knowing? Would the fear and anxiety eventually destroy her?

Throwing off the covers, she slid from bed. Muscles she hadn't used in forever ached, but with a sweet kind of throb that had eased the tension from her body and chased the nightmares away. At least for a little while.

She hurried into the shower, regretting the fact that the inn was empty of guests. At least having to cook breakfast for guests gave her something to do to start the day. Some sense of normalcy when nothing in her life for the past two years had been normal.

Dugan...was he still here?

She quickly showered and threw on some clothes, then dried her hair and pulled it back at the nape of her neck with a clip. Last night had sent them hunting down a false lead.

But today might provide another lead to pursue. She firmly tacked her mental resolve into place.

Rejuvenated by the night of mind-blowing sex, she pulled on boots and hurried to the kitchen. A pot of coffee was half-full and still warm. She poured herself a cup, then searched the living area for Dugan, but he wasn't inside.

Had he left? Why hadn't he told her?

She took her coffee to the back porch and found him there in one of the rocking chairs. He looked rumpled, his beard growth from the day before rough and thick, his eyes shadowed from lack of sleep.

"Have you been out here all night?"

"Off and on."

She sipped her coffee and sank onto the porch swing, using her feet to launch it into a gentle sway. "Why did you leave the bed?"

Silence, thick and filled with regret, stretched between them for a full minute before he spoke. "I offered to do a job, Sage. I shouldn't have slept with you."

True. But his words stung. Still, she sucked up her pride and lifted her chin. "So, what do we do today?"

"Last night I saw a shadow in the woods and came out to check it. Turned out it was a couple of teenagers necking in the woods."

Why was he telling her this? "So?"

"I ran them off, but it started me thinking about the day Lewis crashed."

"I don't get the connection."

"The teenagers tied a boat downstream. They took it back across the creek where they'd probably left a car."

Sage sipped her coffee again, the caffeine finally kick-starting her brain and dragging her mind away from memories of bedding Dugan again.

That was obviously the last thing on his mind.

"Anyway, after the crash, no bodies were found in the fire or anywhere around the area. Which made me start thinking—if Benji is alive and he didn't die with Lewis, who we now know was murdered—how did the shooter escape? As far as I know, the police report didn't mention another car. No skid marks nearby or evidence anyone else had stopped until the accident was called in."

Slowly, Sage began to grasp where he was headed.

"You're thinking that whoever killed Ron escaped on a boat across the creek?"

Dugan shrugged. "It's possible." He stood. "It's also possible that Lewis was meeting someone else. It's just a theory, but let's say that he had reconnected with his first love, Sandra Peyton."

"The woman who'd been pregnant and lost his child."

"Exactly." Dugan stood. "What if she was meeting him and he planned to take Benji to her so they could have the family they'd lost?"

Hope sprouted in Sage's head again.

They had to find Sandra Peyton. But if she had Benji, she probably didn't want to be found.

DUGAN WANTED TO look at that report again, and see the area for himself, so he drove to the sheriff's office.

Sage insisted on accompanying him. Luckily Gandt was out, but the deputy was in. Once Dugan explained that he was helping Sage look for her son, the deputy pulled the file, handed it over and allowed Dugan to make a copy while he returned some phone calls.

"Was there any mention of a boat?" Sage asked as she looked over his shoulder.

"I'm looking." Dugan skimmed the report. The accident had happened at approximately six-forty. A motorist had called it in when she saw the fire shooting up from the bushes.

Sheriff Gandt had arrived along with the fire department, but the car was already burned beyond saving. Once the fire had died down and the rescue workers found no evidence of anyone inside, Gandt organized a search party to comb the area.

During that two-hour interval, Lewis's shooter had escaped.

Dugan spread the photos of the area across the desk

in the front office. Sage made a low, troubled sound as she studied the pictures. The land looked deserted. The weather had been cold that day, patches of dead brush and desolate-looking cacti.

"No boat," Sage said.

"The shooter could have been following Lewis. He caused the crash, then shot Lewis…or he shot him first, causing Lewis to crash."

"If he shot him first, why not let the fire take care of destroying evidence and his body?" Sage asked.

"Because finding the body proves Lewis was murdered, that he didn't die in an accident."

Sage shivered. "If the shooter dragged him out, he must have been bleeding. But I don't see blood in the pictures."

"You're right." Dugan analyzed each one, looking for signs that a body had been dragged from the car, but saw nothing.

He tried to piece together another possibility. What if Lewis had planned to meet someone and fake his death with the car crash? Perhaps whoever it was he'd met had turned on him and shot him.

But why not leave Benji?

Maybe the shooter took Lewis and Benji at gunpoint, shot Lewis, then dumped his body? But again, why take Benji? Because he was a witness?

"Sage, I'd like to go back to the scene and walk the area."

"If you think it'll help."

"Sometimes I work with a dog named Gus. He's an expert tracker dog. Do you have something of Benji's that carries his scent, for Gus to follow?"

Another pained look twisted Sage's face. "Yes."

The deputy was still on the phone, so Dugan mouthed his thanks and they left. He drove to the inn, and Sage hurried inside to get something that had belonged to her son.

SAGE CLUTCHED BENJI'S BLANKET to her and inhaled his sweet scent. Even after two years, it still lingered. She hadn't washed it, and had held on to it for his return, the memory of him cuddling up to it so vivid that it still brought tears to her eyes.

She blinked them back, though, and carried the blanket to Dugan, who was waiting in his SUV.

"He slept with this all the time," Sage said. "I…don't know how he made it past two years without it."

Dugan squeezed her hand as she laid it in her lap. "Hang in there, Sage."

That was the problem. She was hanging on to the hope of finding him alive and bringing him home.

As strong as she pretended to be on the surface, she didn't know if she could handle it if that hope was crushed.

Her mind traveled down that terrifying path that had opened up to her two years ago, to the possibility that he was dead and that they might find his body lying out in the wilderness somewhere. She'd seen the stories on the news and had no idea how parents survived something so horrible.

Dugan drove to his place, a ranch with horses running in the pasture and cattle grazing in the fields, and she forced herself to banish those terrifying images.

"I didn't know you had a working ranch."

Dugan shrugged. "I have a small herd, and I train quarter horses in my spare time."

"And you still have time to consult on cases?"

"Search-and-rescue missions mostly. I have a couple of hired hands, teens from the rez, who help out here."

They climbed out, and she noted the big ranch house. It was a sprawling, rustic log house with a front porch, a house that looked homey and inviting.

A large chocolate Lab raced up and rubbed up against

Dugan's leg. He stooped down and scratched the dog behind his ears. "Hey, Gus. I've got a job for you."

The dog looked up at him as if he understood.

"Did you train him?" Sage asked.

Dugan nodded. "I need to grab a quick shower and change clothes."

Memories of the two of them making love the night before teased her mind, but she reminded herself that he'd stayed with her because someone had tried to kill them, not because he was in love with her.

"Gus, come." Dugan instructed the dog to stay at the front door when they entered, and she noted the Native American artifacts and paintings of nature and horses on the wall. Dark leather furniture, rich pine floors and a floor-to-ceiling stone fireplace made the den feel like a haven.

Dugan disappeared into a back room, and she heard the shower water kick on. She tried not to imagine him naked again, but she couldn't help herself.

Trace and Ron had been good-looking men, but more business types than the rugged, outdoorsy rancher Dugan was.

She spotted a collection of arrowheads on one wall and handwoven baskets on another. But there were no personal touches, no photographs of family or a woman in the house.

She couldn't imagine why a sexy, strong, virile man like Dugan didn't have a woman in his life.

He probably has dozens.

She dismissed the thought. She had to concentrate on finding Benji. When she brought him home, he would need time to acclimate. Like Humpty Dumpty, she'd have to put the pieces of her family back together again.

Dugan appeared, freshly shaven and wearing a clean

shirt and jeans, and nearly took her breath away. Lord help her.

He attached his holster and gun, then settled his Stetson on his head and called for Gus. "Are you ready?" he asked.

She nodded and pushed images of Dugan's sexy body from her mind.

Finding Benji and rebuilding her family was all that mattered.

DUGAN PARKED AT the site of the crash, and they climbed out. He knelt and held Benji's blanket up to the dog to sniff. Gus was the best dog he'd ever had. He had personally trained him, and so far the dog had never let him down. Although with two years having passed, it was doubtful he'd pick up Benji's scent.

Gus took a good sniff, then lowered his nose to the ground and started toward the creek. Dugan followed him, Sage trailing him as Gus sniffed behind bushes and trees and along the creek bank.

But Gus ran up and down the creek, then stopped as if he'd couldn't detect Benji's odor.

Dugan wasn't giving up. He began to comb the area, pushing aside bushes and bramble. Sage followed his cue.

Weeds choked the ground, the dirt dry and hard along the bank. Dugan leaned down to see something in the brush.

A second later, he pulled a tennis shoe from the weeds.

The devastation in Sage's eyes told him the shoe had belonged to her son.

Chapter Seventeen

"That's Benji's shoe." Sage stepped closer. "How did it get in the bushes?"

Dugan didn't want to frighten her with speculations, so he tried to put a positive spin on it. "He could have lost it near the car and an animal found it and carried it here."

Gus sniffed the ground again, and Dugan searched the bushes for the other shoe or any signs of Benji.

Grateful when he didn't find bones, he released a breath. Gus turned the opposite direction and sniffed again, then followed the creek, heading closer to the town and the inn. But again, the time and elements made it impossible to track.

However, they did find an area used for putting boats in and out.

Sage wrung her hands together as she looked across the creek. "Maybe Ron realized he was in trouble, that someone was on to his scam, and he planned to meet that woman Sandra here. Or Carol Sue, one of his other girl-friends or wives?"

Dugan knew she was grasping at straws, but he didn't stop her. "Sounds feasible."

"Maybe he handed Benji off to this woman before he was shot," Sage said.

Dugan shrugged. He doubted that was the case, but he'd be damned if he destroyed Sage's hopes without proof.

They spent another hour coaxing Gus with the blanket and shoe, but they turned up nothing, and Gus kept returning to the site where Dugan thought a boat had been.

The fact that they didn't find Benji's other shoe meant he could have still had it on or that it had floated downstream.

His phone buzzed, and he checked it. Jaxon.

He connected the call. "Yeah?"

"I have an address for Martin's girlfriend, Carol Sue."

"Text it to me."

They hung up and the text came through. Carol Sue lived about forty miles from Cobra Creek.

With no traffic, he could make it there in thirty minutes.

But as he and Sage and Gus headed back to his SUV, he spotted something shiny in the grass. He paused, bent down and brushed a few blades away, then plucked a bullet casing from the ground.

"What is it?" Sage asked.

He held it up to the light. "A bullet. I'll send it to the lab for analysis."

If it was the same one that had shot Lewis, identifying the bullet could lead them to the gun that had shot the man.

And to his killer.

SAGE FOLLOWED DUGAN into the lab, where he dropped off the bullet casing he'd found in the weeds by the creek. He introduced her to Jim Lionheart, who ran the lab.

"It's bent, but it looks like it's from a .38," Lionheart said. "I'll run it. Lots of .38s out there, though. If you bring me a specific gun, I can match it."

"I'm working on it," Dugan said. "Did you see the M.E.'s report on Wilbur Rankins's death?"

Lionheart shook his head no. "You want me to pull it up?"

"I'd appreciate it."

Dugan followed Lionheart to the computer. "Why are you interested in his autopsy?"

"Rankins's grandson called me and said he heard his father and grandfather arguing before he heard the shot."

"You mean his grandson thinks his own father killed his grandfather?" Sage asked.

"He was suspicious. Of course, Gandt didn't even question it."

Lionheart accessed the report, a scowl stretching across his face. "Hmm, odd. Rankins was shot with a handgun. But most of the ranchers around here use rifles or shotguns."

Sage saw the wheels turning in Dugan's head.

"Find out if the bullet I brought in is the same kind that killed Rankins."

"Will do."

"Didn't they do an autopsy?" Sage asked.

"It's standard in a shooting, but I don't think they've ordered one. Since Junior's daddy was dying of cancer anyway and was humiliated by the questions I was asking about the land deals, Junior figured his father just wanted to end the pain."

"I'll call you when I get something."

Dugan thanked him, and Sage walked with him back to his vehicle. "But why would Junior kill Wilbur?" Sage asked. "If he wanted his land, he'd eventually get it."

"Good question," Dugan said. "And one I intend to find the answer to."

QUESTIONS NAGGED AT DUGAN as he drove toward the address he had for Carol Sue. There were too many random pieces to the puzzle, but they had to fit somehow.

If Junior had killed his father, had he also killed Lewis? And why kill his old man if he was going to die and leave him his property, anyway?

The motive for Lewis's murder was clear. Someone—either a woman or a man Lewis had deceived—had gotten revenge by murdering him. If a female had shot him, she'd probably wanted to lash out against him for his lies and betrayal. She might have seen Benji and decided to take him as her own.

On the other hand, if one of the ranchers Lewis had swindled killed him, he wouldn't have wanted the kid. And he certainly couldn't have kept him in Cobra Creek.

There was always the possibility that someone from Lewis's past, another identity Dugan knew nothing about yet, had traced him to Cobra Creek under his new name and shot him.

A half hour later, he turned into a pricey condo development that featured its own stable, tennis courts and country club.

"Carol Sue lives here?" Sage asked.

"That's the address I have. Either she has her own money or Lewis did well when they were together and she benefited."

"Maybe she's just a hardworking woman Ron tried to con."

Dugan stopped at security and identified himself. The guard let him in, and Dugan checked the numbers for the buildings until he found Carol Sue's condo, an end unit at the rear of the complex.

Designated spots were marked for visitors, but each

condo had a built-in garage. He parked, and he and Sage walked up to the door. Dugan punched the doorbell and glanced around, noting that the small lawns were well tended, each unit painted to create a unified feel.

When no one answered, he rang the doorbell again, then stepped to the side to peer in the front window. There was no furniture inside.

"Looks like she's moved out," Dugan said.

Sage sighed. "Are you sure?"

"There's no furniture in the living room. Let me check around back." He descended the brick steps, then walked around the side of the condo. A small fenced-in yard offered privacy, and when he checked the gate, it was unlocked.

Sage followed on his heels as he entered the backyard. The stone patio held no outdoor furniture. He crossed the lawn to the back but the door was locked.

Damn.

He removed a small tool from his pocket, picked the lock, then pushed the door open. The back opened to a narrow entryway with a laundry and mudroom to the left. Sage trailed him as he stepped into a modern kitchen with granite counters and stainless steel appliances.

"There's no table." Sage opened a few cabinet doors. "No food or dishes, either. You're right. She's gone."

A noise sounded upstairs. Footsteps?

Dugan pulled his weapon and motioned for Sage to move behind him. Then he crept through the hallway. He checked the living and dining area. Both empty.

The footsteps sounded again. Then a woman appeared on the stairs. She threw up her hands and screamed when she saw them.

She was dressed in heels and a dress and wasn't armed, so he lowered his gun.

"Sorry, ma'am. Are you Carol Sue?"

The woman fluttered her hand over her heart, visibly shaken. "No, I'm Tanya Willis, the real estate broker for the development. Who are you?"

Dugan identified himself and introduced Sage. "We're looking for Carol Sue."

"I have no idea where she is," the woman said. "Why do you want to see her?"

"We think she was connected to a man, Ron Lewis, whose body was recently found in Cobra Creek. Carol Sue knew him by another name, though, Mike Martin."

Tanya gasped and gripped the stair rail. "You said Mike was murdered?"

"Yes, ma'am," Dugan replied.

Sage stepped up beside him. "He also took my little boy, Benji, with him the day he was killed. You may have seen the story on the news."

"Oh, my God, yes." Tanya swept one hand over her chest. "You think Carol Sue had something to do with that man's murder and your little boy's disappearance?"

"That's what we're trying to discern." Dugan paused. "Does Carol Sue own the condo?"

"Yes," Tanya said. "She was so excited when she first bought the place and moved in. Told me she'd never had a nice home before, and that her boyfriend had a windfall and they were planning to get married and live here together."

"When was that?"

"A little over three years ago," Tanya said. "I stopped to see her a couple of times after that, thought I'd meet her fiancé since he sounded so wonderful, but both times she said he was out of town."

"Her boyfriend's windfall was due to the fact that he was a con artist," Dugan said.

Again, the real estate broker looked shocked.

"When did Carol Sue move out?" Sage asked.

"Just a couple of days ago," Tanya said. "That was weird, too. She called me and said she had to relocate and wanted me to handle putting the unit on the market."

Dugan traded looks with Sage. Had the discovery of Lewis's body prompted her quick departure?

"Did she say why she had to relocate?" Sage asked.

Tanya shook her head, her lower lip trembling. "No, but she definitely sounded upset. Like she might be afraid of something."

Dugan considered that comment. Had Carol Sue been upset because she'd learned Lewis was dead and feared his killer might come after her? Or because she'd killed him and didn't want to get caught?

Or had the publicity about the murder and Benji's disappearance made her run because she had Sage's son?

SAGE TWISTED HER HANDS together as they left the condo complex. Dugan phoned his friend Jaxon, with the rangers, and relayed what they'd learned about Carol Sue.

Sage's cell phone buzzed, and she checked the number. An unknown.

Curious, she hit Answer. "Hello."

"You need to stop nosing around."

A chill swept up her spine. It was a woman's voice this time. "Who is this?"

"It doesn't matter who it is. If you don't stop, you're going to end up dead."

The phone clicked silent.

Sage's hand trembled as she lowered the phone to her lap.

"Who was that?" Dugan asked.

"I don't know," Sage said, shaken and angry at the same time. "A woman. She warned me to stop nosing around or I'd end up dead."

Dugan checked her phone. An unknown number. Probably a burner phone, but he called Jaxon to get a trace put on Sage's phone in case the caller phoned again.

When he hung up, he turned to Sage, trying to make sense of everything. "First, a man breaks in and threatens you. And now a woman calls with threats. They must be working together."

"Do you think it was Carol Sue?"

"Could be. Or it could have been Sandra Peyton."

"But if Sandra met up with Ron before he died and took Benji, who is the man?"

"I don't know," Dugan said. "As far as we know, Sandra had nothing to do with the land scams in Cobra Creek."

What if Sandra had reconnected with Ron and they'd planned to con the people in Cobra Creek, then disappear with the money?

If so, did she have Benji with her?

HE WAS CLOSE on Carol Sue's tail. The damn woman thought she'd get away, but she was wrong.

He had to tie up all loose ends.

He held back in his car, following her at a safe distance, careful not to tip her off. She'd been hiding out since Lewis disappeared.

But she'd tried to blackmail him first.

He didn't kowtow to blackmail from anyone.

Not that she had understood what was going on, but she knew enough.

Too much.

She swerved the little sedan into the motel, parked at the front and rushed inside, scanning the parking lot and checking over her shoulder as if she sensed she was being followed.

Stupid broad. She'd gotten greedy.

Now she would pay.

He parked to the side and waited until she rushed out

with the key. She moved her car down the row of rooms to the last one at the end.

He grinned as she grabbed her bag and hurried inside the room.

Laughter bubbled in his chest.

Night was falling, but it wasn't dark enough to strike just yet. The motel backed up to a vacant warehouse parking lot. There he might stick out.

Better to blend in with the crowd, so he parked a few spaces down in front of a room with no lights on, indicating it was vacant. Satisfied she'd tucked in for the evening, he walked across the street to the bar/diner.

He slid into a back booth and ordered a burger and beer but kept a low profile as he enjoyed his meal. Night had descended by the time he finished, but he wanted to wait another half hour to give the bar time to fill up so no one would notice him leaving.

So he ordered a piece of apple pie and coffee and took his time.

His belly full, he paid the bill in cash, then stepped outside for a smoke. The first drag gave him a nicotine buzz, and he stayed in the shadows of the bar until he finished and tossed the cigarette butt to the ground. He stomped it in the dirt with his boot, then walked back across the street.

Still, he waited, watching her room until she flipped off the lights. He gave her time to get to sleep, then slid from his car and eased down the row of rooms until he reached hers.

He quickly picked the lock, then inched inside. The soles of his shoes barely made any noise as he walked toward the bed. She lay curled beneath the blanket on her side, one hand resting beneath her face.

He grabbed a pillow from the chair, then leaned over her. Her eyes popped open, and she started to scream when she saw him.

But he shoved the pillow over her face and held it down, pressing it over her nose and mouth. She struggled, kicked and clawed at him, but he was stronger and used his weight to smother the life out of her.

Even after her limbs went still and her body limp, he kept the pillow on her for another two minutes to make sure she was dead.

He didn't want her returning to haunt him and ruin all he'd done to get where he was.

In fact, he'd kill anyone who got in his way.

Including Sage Freeport and that damn Indian, who were asking questions all over Cobra Creek.

Chapter Eighteen

Dugan's phone buzzed as he drove back to Cobra Creek.

"Mr. Graystone," Donnell said, his voice hesitant.

"Yes. What can I do for you, Mr. Earnest?"

"I've been thinking about what you said that day, about my ranch and that Lewis jerk."

"Go on."

"I heard Wilbur Rankins is dead."

"That's true. The sheriff said he shot himself because of the truth about the scam coming out."

A tense moment passed. Earnest cleared his throat. "Listen to me, mister. I don't know what the hell's going on, but I do know Wilbur. That man was the most prideful man I've ever known. Sure, he would have hated being showed up by some bigwig stranger that duped him out of his land, but he would never kill himself. *Never.*"

"What makes you so sure?"

"First of all, he loved his grandson too damn much. He always said suicide was a coward's way out. His daddy took his own life, and Wilbur hated him for it."

Interesting. "What about his cancer? If he was in a lot of pain, maybe he committed suicide to keep his family from watching him suffer or to keep them from paying medical bills."

Earnest mumbled a crude remark. "He might have been

worried about money and bills, but he just got a report saying he was doing better. He thought he was going to beat that cancer after all."

Dugan stifled a surprised response. That wasn't the impression he'd gotten. "Do you know who his doctor was?"

"Doc Moser sent him to some specialist oncologist in San Antonio."

"What is it you want me to do?" Dugan asked.

A long sigh echoed back. "Find out the truth. If Wilbur didn't kill himself, then someone murdered him. And if it has to do with the land, I'm worried they're gonna come after me."

Dugan scrubbed his hand over his neck. That was a possibility. "Thanks for calling, Mr. Earnest. I'll let you know what I find."

When he hung up, Sage was watching him, so he relayed the conversation. Then he turned the SUV in the direction of the doctor's office in Cobra Creek.

BY THE TIME they reached Cobra Creek, the doctor's office was closed.

"Do you know where he lives?" Dugan asked.

"Two houses down from the inn."

She pointed out Dr. Moser's house, and Dugan parked. "Do you know him?"

Sage nodded. "He's the only doctor around. He treated me and Benji."

Dr. Moser's house was a two story with flower boxes in front and a garden surrounded by a wrought-iron fence in back. His wife apparently spent hours tending her flowers.

Sage rang the bell while Dugan glanced up and down the street. A moment later, Mrs. Moser, graying hair and a kind smile, opened the door and greeted them.

Sage introduced Dugan and explained that he was helping her look for her son. "Can we come in?" Sage asked. "We need to talk to Dr. Moser."

The doctor appeared behind her, adjusting his bifocals. "Hello, Sage. Is something wrong?"

"Please let us come in and we'll explain," she said.

Mrs. Moser waved them in and offered coffee, but they declined. The doctor gestured toward the living room, and they seated themselves.

Dugan began. "I suppose you heard that Ron Lewis's body was found by the creek."

Dr. Moser nodded. "I did hear that. Saw Dr. Longmire yesterday, and he told me that Lewis was shot."

"Yes, he was," Dugan said.

Dr. Moser gave Sage a sympathetic look. "I'm sorry. I heard they still haven't found Benji."

Sage folded her hands and acknowledged his comment with a small nod.

"So what brought you here?" Dr. Moser asked.

Dugan explained about Lewis's scam. "I have reason to suspect that Wilbur Rankins might not have killed himself."

Dr. Moser pulled a hand down his chin. "I don't understand. I'm not the medical examiner."

"No, but you can answer one question. Sheriff Gandt said that Rankins shot himself because he was ashamed that he'd been duped by Lewis and because he was dying of cancer."

Dr. Moser looked back and forth between them. "He did have cancer. But you know the HIPAA law prevents me from discussing his medical condition."

"Dr. Moser," Dugan said bluntly. "The man is dead. In fact, he may have been murdered. All I need to know is if his condition was terminal or if he was going to get better."

Indecision warred in the doctor's eyes for a moment,

then he leaned forward in his chair. "I do believe he'd just learned that the chemo was working."

Sage sucked in a sharp breath. If he'd just received a good prognosis, it didn't make sense that he'd take his own life.

DUGAN THANKED THE DOCTOR, Donnell Earnest's suspicions echoing in his head. Was Earnest right? Had someone murdered Rankins?

Someone who'd partnered with Lewis?

He drove toward the bank, wondering if Bates had any insight. "When Lewis was with you, did he ever mention a partner?"

Sage rubbed her temple. "Not that I remember."

"How about the name of the developer?"

She closed her eyes as if in thought. "It was something like Woodard or Woodfield. No, Woodsman. I remember thinking that it suited the business."

"We need to research it." Dugan parked at the bank, and he and Sage entered together.

"While you talk to Mr. Bates, I'm going to talk to Delores," Sage said. "She's the loan officer here. Maybe she knows something."

"Good idea." Dugan strode toward Bates's office while Sage veered to the right to speak to her friend.

When he knocked, Bates called for him to come in. The man looked slightly surprised to see him but gestured for him to sit down.

"What can I do for you today, Mr. Graystone?" Bates asked.

"Who was this developer working with Lewis?"

Bates tugged at his tie, nervous. "The company name was Woodsman."

"What about Junior? Does he know this?"

"Yes. Junior is irate. He was furious with his father for signing with Lewis in the first place."

So Junior might have killed his father...

Or someone from the company could have killed Rankins to keep him from challenging the legitimacy of the deal.

Dugan thanked him and phoned Jaxon as he left the man's office. He had to find the person behind Woodsman.

SAGE KNEW DELORES from the bank and church. In fact, Delores had helped her with her loan for the renovations with the inn when she first decided to buy and refurbish it. They had become friendly enough for an occasional lunch and social gathering.

Until Benji disappeared. Then she'd shut down and kept to herself.

Delores waved to her from her desk. "Hey, Sage. How are you?"

"Can we talk in private?" Sage asked.

Delores's eyebrows shot up, but she gestured toward the door to her office. Jingle bells tinkled on it as Sage closed it. She sank into one of the chairs opposite her friend's desk, noting a Christmas tin full of cookies and candy canes.

"What's going on?" Delores asked. "I heard that Dugan Graystone found Ron Lewis's body."

Sage knew some of the residents in town weren't as friendly to the people from the reservation as they should be, an archaic attitude that she had no tolerance for. Dugan seemed to travel between both worlds fairly well. Most of the single women in town were intrigued by his dark, sexy physique and those haunted bedroom eyes.

But the men were standoffish.

Normally she didn't listen to gossip, but occasionally, a grain of truth could be found beneath the murk. "What are they saying?"

"That he was murdered," Delores said in a low voice as if she thought someone might be listening.

"He was shot," Sage said.

"Do they know who did it?"

"No, but Dugan Graystone is investigating."

Delores thumbed her auburn hair over her shoulder. "That's why he's here?"

"Yes," Sage said. "He's also helping me look for Benji."

"Yes, that's what they said on the news." Delores sighed. "You don't think…?" She cut herself off as she realized the ugly implications. "I'm sorry, Sage. I know this must be horrible for you."

"It has been," Sade admitted. "That's why I want to talk to you. Ron Lewis wasn't really who he said he was. He was a fraud who conned people out of their land. Ron said that he worked for this developer by the name of Woodsman. Do you know anything about that company?"

Delores wrinkled her nose. "No. Although that name sounds familiar." She turned and tapped some keys on the computer, her frown deepening. "I shouldn't be telling you this, but that name does show up on an account here."

Sage leaned forward. "Do you have any more information about the person who opened the account?"

Delores tapped a few more keys, a look of frustration tightening the lines around her eyes. "Hmm."

"What is it?"

"Let me look into something."

Sage drummed her fingers on her leg as she waited while Delores worked her magic. Her friend had confided once that she was somewhat of a hacker.

Delores sighed, long and meaningful, into the silence. "Oh, this is interesting."

"What?"

"I think Woodsman might be a dummy corporation."

"One Ron Lewis set up so he could personally hide money he was stealing from landowners."

Delores nodded, although her face paled as she looked at Sage. "That's not all. There's one other person who has access to the money in that account."

Sage's mind raced. It had to be someone at the bank who'd figured out what was going on. "You mean Mr. Bates?"

Delores shook her head no. "Sheriff Gandt."

DUGAN'S PHONE BUZZED as he left Bates's office. "Graystone."

"It's Jaxon. Meet me at the motel outside Cobra Creek."

"What's going on?"

"The cleaning staff found a body in one of the rooms."

"I'll be there ASAP."

He waited outside Delores's office for Sage. Her complexion looked a pasty-gray as she exited the office.

"Sage?"

She motioned for him to walk with her, and they left the bank. She didn't speak until they'd settled into his SUV.

"What did your friend say?"

Sage heaved a wary breath. "Delores looked up the account for Woodsman."

"And?"

"There was another person attached to the account." She turned to him, her expression etched in turmoil. "You won't believe who it was."

Dugan's patience was stretched thin. "Who?"

"The sheriff."

Dugan muttered a curse. "So Gandt was working with Lewis?"

Sage shrugged. "It looks like that. I guess the question is whether or not Gandt knew Ron was running a con, and if he was in on it."

Chapter Nineteen

Dugan should have been shocked at the fact that Gandt's name was associated with the account, but he'd never liked the bastard, so shock wasn't a factor.

But he drove to the motel, furious at the idea that the man who was supposed to be protecting and taking care of the town might be dirty. And that he might have taken advantage of the very people who'd trusted him and voted him into office.

"Do you think the sheriff knew what Ron was up to?" Sage asked, almost as if she was struggling to face the fact that Gandt might have lied to her.

"That arrogant SOB thinks he owns this town. I wouldn't put it past him to join in on a scheme that would garner him a bigger part of the pie."

Dugan spotted Jaxon's car in front of the motel room at the far end, room eight, swung his SUV into the lot and parked.

"What are we doing here?"

"Jaxon called. A body was found here."

Sage's mouth twitched downward. "Oh, God. Who is it?"

"We'll find out." Dugan reached for the door and opened it, then walked around to Sage's door, but she was already out. He was amazed at the strength she emanated.

When they reached the motel room, a uniformed officer met them where he stood guard. Dugan identified himself, and Jaxon walked up.

"Wait outside, Sage," Dugan told her.

He followed Jaxon across the room where Sheriff Gandt stood by the body of a woman on the bed. The M.E. was stooped beside her, conducting an exam.

"Have you identified her?" Dugan asked Jaxon.

Jaxon nodded. "Found a wallet in her car outside, with her license. Her name is Carol Sue Tinsley. That's why I thought you'd be interested."

"Damn." He'd halfway hoped they would find her and Benji together.

Sheriff Gandt glared at him. "What are you doing here?"

"I phoned him," Jaxon said. "This woman had a prior relationship with the man you knew as Ron Lewis."

Gandt's thick eyebrows shot up. "How do you know that?"

"I'm a Texas Ranger," Jaxon said, a sharp bite to his tone. "It's my job to investigate murders and kidnappings."

Dugan almost grinned. He knew Jaxon well enough to understand the implied message, that it was his job to step in when incompetence reigned.

"What was cause of death?" Dugan asked.

The M.E. was conducting a liver temp test. "The petechial hemorrhaging in the eyes suggests asphyxiation." He used his fingers to lift her eyelids, one at a time.

Dugan glanced at the pillow on the floor by the bed. Probably the murder weapon.

No bullet this time.

Was she murdered by the same perp who'd shot Lewis? If so, why a different MO?

To throw off the police?

"Have you found any forensics evidence?" Dugan asked.

Gandt shook his head. "I searched the room, but no signs of who did this."

"Any sexual assault?" Dugan asked.

Dr. Longmire shook his head. "None." He pulled the sheet back to reveal that she was still clothed in flannel pajamas. "My guess is she was sleeping when she was attacked."

"Was anyone with her when she checked in?" Dugan asked.

"No." Jaxon rubbed his chin. "Her car was registered to the name on her driver's license. But at the registration desk, she signed in as Camilla Anthony."

"So she was hiding from someone."

"Or meeting a lover," Sheriff Gandt said.

Dugan scoffed. "Most women don't wear flannel pj's to a romantic rendezvous."

Jaxon murmured agreement. "I'm going to canvass the other rooms in case another guest saw something."

The M.E. lifted one of her hands, indicating a broken nail. "It looks like she put up a fight. I'll see if I can get DNA."

"Even a thread of her attacker's clothing could help," Dugan added.

The sheriff shifted, walked over and bent to study the body. "I still think she was probably running from an ex-boyfriend. Maybe he followed her here, waited till she went to bed, then slipped in and choked her."

"What about the lock?" Dugan asked.

"It was picked," Jaxon said. "So far, no prints."

"And her belongings?" Dugan asked.

"We found a suitcase," Jaxon said. "Clothing, shoes, toiletries. I searched her purse, but no indication where she was headed. No map or papers with any kind of address on it."

"Money?"

"She did have a stash of cash, nearly a thousand dollars," Jaxon said.

"So robbery was not a motive." Dugan chewed over that information, then turned to Gandt. "Did you know this woman, Sheriff?"

Gandt hitched up his pants. "No, why would I?"

Dugan studied the way the man's mouth twitched. "Because she was Lewis's girlfriend when he went by the name of Mike Martin."

"That so?"

"Yes," Dugan said. "He had a string of names he used for his other scams."

Gandt crossed his beefy arms. "What else have you found out about Lewis?"

"He has a rap sheet for arrests under three different names for fraud and embezzlement. And he conned some local ranchers in Cobra Creek." Dugan glanced at Jaxon. "Did you find a cell phone in her purse or car?"

Jaxon shook his head no. "If she had one, the killer must have taken it."

To cover his tracks.

Dugan turned and scrutinized the room. The neon lights of a dive bar flickered against the night sky. "While you sweep the room for forensics, I may take a walk over there." Dugan turned to the sheriff. "Like you said, if the killer was watching her, he might have gone inside to wait until he thought she was asleep."

The sheriff tugged at his pants. "I'll do that," he said in a tone that brooked no argument. "I'm the law around here, Graystone, and don't you forget it."

He was the law. But Dugan didn't trust him worth a damn, especially now that he knew Gandt's name was associated with the account related to the land deals.

Could Gandt have killed Lewis so he could gain access

to the property and money for himself? So he really could own Cobra Creek?

And what about Carol Sue? Maybe she'd traced Lewis to Cobra Creek and come looking for Lewis or her share of whatever money she thought he owed her.

SAGE PACED OUTSIDE the motel room, anxious to know what was going on inside.

Finally Dugan stepped out with a tall muscular man in a Stetson wearing a Texas Ranger badge on his shirt. Dugan introduced him as his friend Jaxon, and Sage thanked him for his help.

"Who was the woman?" Sage asked.

"Carol Sue," Dugan said with an apologetic look.

Disappointment ripped through Sage. If Carol Sue had any information about Benji, she couldn't tell them now.

"She was smothered," Dugan continued. "She put up a fight, though, so hopefully the M.E. can extract DNA from underneath her fingernails."

"I'm going to talk to the other guests at the motel," Jaxon said. "Maybe we'll find a witness."

"Let's divide up and it'll go faster." Dugan touched Sage's elbow. "Will you be okay here?"

"Sure, go ahead."

Jaxon headed to the first unit while Dugan took the one next to the room where the woman lay dead.

Sheriff Gandt stepped outside. "Did you know the woman in there, Ms. Freeport?"

"No," Sage said. "Did you?"

The sheriff's eyebrows drew together, creating frown lines across his forehead. "No. She's not from Cobra Creek."

"What do you think she was doing here?" Sage asked.

Sheriff Gandt shrugged and made a noncommittal

sound. "Looks like she was probably meeting a lover. They had a quarrel and he killed her."

"Still, it seems odd that she was in Cobra Creek," Sage countered. "Especially so soon after Ron Lewis's body was found."

"You think she came here looking for his killer?" Gandt asked in a skeptical tone. "Hell, it's been two years since he disappeared."

"She probably saw the news of his death and wanted to talk to you about it," Sage suggested.

The sheriff's mouth twitched. "I guess that's possible."

"You also had connections to the land deal Ron had put together."

Shock widened Gandt's eyes. "Who the hell told you that?"

"It doesn't matter who told me," Sage said curtly. "What matters is that you were in cahoots with Ron to buy up the land around Cobra Creek. You were swindling your own people."

A dark rage flashed in the sheriff's eyes. "You don't know what you're talking about, Ms. Freeport."

"I know that you never really tried to find my son." Sage was spitting mad. "And that your name is associated with the developer Ron was working with." She planted her hands on her hips. "And that you could have killed him so you'd get all the money and land yourself."

"I'd be really careful about making accusations, Ms. Freeport," he said with a growl. "I'd hate to see you end up like that woman in there."

Sage's heart hammered in her chest. Was he threatening her?

The motel held twelve rooms, but only half of them were occupied.

The first door Dugan knocked on held an elderly couple

who claimed they hadn't seen or heard anything because they'd retreated to bed as soon as it got dark. Apparently they'd both grown up on a farm, and they rose with the roosters and went to bed with the sun.

He moved to the next room and knocked on the door. A minute later, a young man in jeans and a cowboy hat opened the door. He pulled off headphones from his ears. "Yeah?"

"I'm sorry to bother you, but there was a woman murdered in room eight. We're asking everyone in the motel if they saw or heard anything."

The guy gestured toward his guitar, which was propped against the bed. Two young guys in their twenties also sat in a circle with a banjo and fiddle, and a brunette was strumming chords on her own guitar.

"Afraid not. We were jamming, working on some new material."

"Are you guys from around here?"

"North Texas. We're on our way to Nashville for a gig."

Dugan gestured toward the others. "Did any of you see someone near room eight?"

A chorus of nos rumbled through the room. "I thought I heard some banging," the girl said. "But I figured it was someone getting it on."

This group was no help. Dugan didn't see any reason to collect their contact information, but he laid a card on the dresser. "Call me if you remember anything. Maybe a car or person lurking around."

He tried the door next to them, but a family with twin toddlers answered the door. "Sorry, we went to dinner and drove around to see the Christmas lights," the father said. "By the time we returned, the sheriff's car was already outside."

Dugan thanked them, then moved down the row of rooms. But it was futile. Barring the cars and trucks in the lot, which were all accounted for by guests, no one had witnessed anything.

His phone buzzed against his hip, and he checked the number. Unknown.

He quickly connected the call. "Dugan Graystone."

"I have some information about Ron Lewis."

Dugan clenched the phone and looked around the parking lot in case the caller was nearby. "Who is this?"

"Meet me at Hangman's Bridge. An hour."

The voice was blurred, low, hoarse. Disguised.

"I'll be there." He hung up and checked his watch for the time. It could be a setup.

But it could be the tip he needed to end the case and find Benji.

NERVES KNOTTED SAGE's shoulders as she and Dugan walked across the street to the bar.

"The canvass of the motel turned up nothing."

Sage sighed. "The sheriff warned me not to go around making accusations against him."

Dugan's eyes flared with anger. "Bastard. He's in this. I just need to prove it."

Sage still couldn't believe it. She had turned to Sheriff Gandt two years ago and even trusted him at first. Sure, she'd been frustrated that he hadn't found Benji, but it had never occurred to her that he might have been involved in her son's disappearance.

Even if he had killed Ron, why would he do something to Benji? As sheriff, he could have covered up the murder, then returned Benji to her and looked like a hero.

The bar was dark and smoky as they entered. Dugan had snapped a picture of Carol Sue and showed it to the hostess. "Do you recognize this woman?"

She shook her head. "What's going on?"

Dugan relayed the fact that Carol Sue had been murdered in the room across the street. "Was she in here earlier?"

"I didn't see her," the hostess said. She waved the bartender over. "Lou, was this woman in here earlier tonight?"

Lou dried his hands on a towel. "Naw. She ain't been in."

Dugan explained about the murder. "It's possible that her killer came in," Dugan said. "Did you notice anyone suspicious? Maybe someone who seemed nervous? He might have watched the door or checked the time."

"All that's been in tonight is the regulars," Lou said. "Well, 'cept for this group of young folks, said they was in a band."

"We talked to them." Dugan handed them each a card. "If you think of anything, no matter how small, please give me a call."

Sage and Dugan walked back outside to the SUV. An ambulance had arrived to transport Carol Sue's body back to the morgue for an autopsy. Sage looked up and saw Sheriff Gandt lift his head and pin her with his intimidating stare.

Dugan's expression was grim as he drove her back to the inn. Night had set in long ago and exhaustion pulled at her limbs. And it was another day closer to Christmas.

And still no Benji.

The memory of Dugan's arms around her taunted her, making her yearn to have him make love to her again. To comfort her and chase her nightmarish fears away for a few more hours.

But after he searched the inn, he paused at the door.

"An anonymous caller phoned that he has information about Lewis," Dugan said. "Lock the doors, Sage, and stay inside until I get back."

She nodded, then watched him leave. Too antsy to sleep, she combed the inn.

A knock sounded at the door, and she rushed to answer it. The sheriff stood on the other side.

"Sheriff?"

"Come with me, Ms. Freeport. I may have a lead on your son."

Sage's heart stuttered. After the visit at the bank, she didn't know whether or not to trust him.

"Let me call Dugan to go with us."

"That's not necessary," Sheriff Gandt said.

"But—"

Her words were cut off as he raised his gun and slammed it against her skull.

Pain ricocheted through her temple, and then the world went black.

Chapter Twenty

Dugan parked in the woods by Hangman's Bridge, his instincts on alert. The fact that the anonymous caller had chosen this area to meet aroused his suspicions.

It was called Hangman's Bridge for a reason—two teenagers had died in a suicide pact by hanging themselves from the old metal bridge.

He pulled his gun, surveying the trees and area surrounding the bridge, looking for movement. An animal howled from somewhere close by, and the sound of leaves crunching crackled in the air.

He spun to the right at the sharp sound of twigs snapping. Then a gunshot blasted. Dugan ducked and darted behind an oak to avoid being hit.

Another shot pinged off the tree, shattering bark. He opened fire in the direction from where the bullet had come from, searching the darkness.

The silhouette of a man lurked by the bridge, the shadow of his hat catching Dugan's eye. Dugan crept behind another tree, careful to keep his footfalls light so as not to alert the man that he'd spotted him.

Another shot flew toward him, and he darted beneath the rusted metal rungs of the bridge and returned fire. His bullet sailed into the bushes near the man, then leaves rustled as the gunman shifted to run.

Dugan raced from one hiding spot to another, quickly closing the distance, and snuck up behind the man just before he ran for his truck in a small clearing to the left.

Dugan tackled the guy from behind, slamming him down into the brush. The man struggled, but his gun slipped from his hand and fell into a patch of dried leaves and branches.

They wrestled on the ground as the bastard tried to retrieve it, and the man managed to knock Dugan off him for a second. Dugan scrambled back to his feet as the shooter jumped up to run. But Dugan lunged toward him, caught him around the shoulders and spun him around.

Lloyd Riley.

"Riley," Dugan said. "Give it up."

But Lloyd swung a fist toward Dugan and connected with his jaw. A hard right.

Dugan grunted and returned a blow, the two of them trading one after the other until Dugan kicked Riley in the kneecap and sent him collapsing to the ground with a bellow of pain.

Dugan kicked him again, this time a sharp foot to the solar plexus, rendering him helpless.

Riley curled into a ball, hugging his leg. "You broke my damn kneecap!"

"You're lucky you're alive." Dugan flipped the big man over, pressed one foot into Riley's lower back to hold him still while he jerked his arms behind him, yanked a piece of rope from his pocket and tied his wrists together.

Riley growled an obscenity into the dirt. Dugan rolled him over and shoved his gun into his face.

"Why the hell were you shooting at me?"

Riley's lips curled into a hiss. "I had to," he muttered.

Dugan gripped Riley's shirt collar, yanking it tightly to choke the man. "What does that mean?"

Blood trickled down Riley's forehead near his left eye,

another line seeping from the corner of his mouth. Then Dugan noticed the leather tassel on Riley's gloves. One was missing.

"You damn bastard, you broke into Sage Freeport's bedroom and tried to strangle her."

"I'm not talking till I get a lawyer."

Dugan laughed, a bitter sound. "You will talk to me. I'm not the law, Riley." He shoved the gun deeper into the man's cheek. "Now, why were you trying to kill me?"

Riley's Adam's apple bobbed as he swallowed hard.

"Spit it out," Dugan snarled.

"Gandt told me to."

Dugan's stomach knotted. "What?"

"That Freeport broad found out he was in cahoots with Lewis, and he knew you were on to him."

"So it's true, Gandt and Lewis were working together?"

"Not at first," Riley said. "But Gandt figured out Lewis was a con man and wanted in."

"Then he got greedy and killed Lewis so he could have the land to himself."

Riley nodded. "He told me I could keep my ranch if I helped cover for him."

"If you killed me?" Dugan asked.

Riley spit blood from his mouth. "He said he'd frame me for killing Lewis. Then I'd lose my ranch and go to jail."

"What about the driver of that car that ran me and Sage off the road?"

Riley's face twisted with pain. "He was one of my hired hands."

Dugan gripped the man's collar tighter. "Where is Gandt now?"

Riley averted his eyes, and Dugan cursed. "Where is he?"

"He went after the Freeport woman. Said if I took care of you, he'd take care of her."

Dugan went stone-cold still. He had to get to Sage.

Sage stirred from unconsciousness, the world a dark blur. What had happened? Where was she?

Gandt... God, the sheriff had been in on the scam. And now he had her....

And he was going to kill her.

She had to find a way out, call Dugan. Make the sheriff confess what he'd done with Benji.

She blinked to clear her vision, then realized she was tied to a chair, her hands bound behind her back, her feet bound at the ankles. She struggled to untie the knot at her wrists as she searched the darkness.

The scent of hay and horses suffused the air. She must be in a barn. But whose?

The sheriff didn't own a ranch...did he?

Maybe it was one of the properties he'd confiscated through the phony land deals.

But which one? And where was he now?

The squeak of the barn door startled her, and she whipped her head to the side and saw a shadowy figure in the doorway.

"What are you going to do, kill me, too?" Sage shouted.

His footsteps crushed the hay on the floor as he walked toward her. A sliver of moonlight seeped through the barn door where it was cracked, painting his face a murky gray.

"I warned you not to keep poking around," Gandt said in a menacing tone. "You should have listened."

Still struggling with the ropes behind her back, Sage clenched her teeth. "Where is my son?"

Gandt lumbered toward her, tugging at his pants. His gun glinted in the dark as he trained it on her. "I don't know."

Sage's heart raced. "What do you mean, you don't know?"

His scowl deepened, a muscle ticking in his jaw. "When I got to Lewis that night, he was alone."

Sage's head throbbed from where he'd slammed the butt

of the gun against her temple, but she gritted her teeth at the nausea. "You're lying. We found Benji's shoe by the creek near the crash site."

Gandt waved the gun around. "I'm telling you the kid was already gone when I met up with Lewis."

Fear engulfed Sage. He had to be lying. "I don't believe you. Benji had to be with Ron."

Gandt cursed. "Listen, Ms. Freeport, I'm telling you, he wasn't. Lewis must have dropped him off before he came to meet me."

"You were going to meet him about the land?"

"Yeah," Gandt said with a smirk. "You think I'm not smart enough to figure out what he was doing?" He paced in front of her, his jowls jiggling. "Well, I am. Once I talked to a couple of locals and they told me he'd offered to buy up their property, I started looking into him. Ain't nobody messin' with my town."

Sage almost had one end of the rope through the back loop. "So you blackmailed him for a cut of the money?"

"I wanted that land," Gandt said. "First off, he said no way, but I can be convincing."

"You killed him, didn't you?" Sage's stomach rolled. "Then you forged papers so you could take over the rancher's properties."

"Hell, they'd rather be beholden to me than let some stranger turn their ranches into shopping malls and those damn coffee shops."

He lit a cigarette, then lifted it and took a drag. The ashes sparkled against the dark.

"Then that Indian friend of yours had to find Lewis's body, and you started nosing around."

Panic seized Sage. "All I want is my son. Just tell me where he is, and I promise I won't tell anyone what you did to Ron."

A dark laugh rumbled from Gandt. "Sure you won't.

You talked to people at the bank. You went to the stinking press."

Tears burned the backs of Sage's eyes. "Please, just tell me. Is Benji all right?"

Gandt blew smoke through his nostrils, smoke rings floating in the air between them. "I told you the truth. I don't know what happened to the boy."

Sage struggled to understand. Could he have been in the car when they crashed and ran when he saw Gandt? "What happened?"

"I set fire to the car to cover up the murder. And it would have worked if you hadn't come along asking questions."

Sage's mind tried to piece together the facts. Had Ron left Benji with someone else when he went to meet the sheriff? Maybe one of the women from his past?

Not Carol Sue—she was dead.

Sandra Peyton…

Her conversation with Maude Handleman, then Janelle Dougasville echoed in her head. Sandra had lost Ron's baby, and so had Maude. And Janelle said he'd never had a real family.

Was that what Ron was chasing? The reason he'd chosen her in the first place, so he could take Benji and raise him with Sandra, his first love?

Frantically she worried with the ropes, but the sheriff inhaled another drag from his cigarette, then dropped it onto the floor of the barn. She gasped as the embers sparked and a blade of hay caught fire.

Gandt leered at her and backed toward the door, and fear paralyzed her. He was going to burn down the barn with her in it.

DUGAN CALLED SAGE, panicked that Gandt had hurt her. Her phone trilled and trilled, his heart hammering as he waited to hear her voice.

But on the fifth ring, it rolled to voice mail. "Sage, the sheriff is dirty. If he shows up, don't open the door. And call me so I know you're okay."

He ended the call, then punched her number again, but once more he got her machine.

Dugan jerked Riley up and hauled him to his SUV. "Where would Gandt take Sage?"

Riley's eyes bulged. "I don't know."

Dugan shook him hard. "Tell me, dammit. If he hurts her, you're going down for it, too."

"I told you I don't know," Riley bellowed. "He ordered me to take care of you and said he'd handle her."

Dugan wanted to kill him on the spot. But he had to find Sage.

He searched Riley for another weapon, but he was clean, so he shoved him into the backseat. For a brief moment, he considered calling the deputy, but the deputy might be in cahoots with Gandt.

Jaxon was the only one he trusted.

He reached for his phone and started to shut Riley's door, but Riley's phone buzzed from his pocket.

Maybe it was Gandt, checking in.

Riley frowned as Dugan retrieved the rancher's phone from his shirt pocket.

Dammit, not Gandt.

He flipped it around to show Riley the name on the caller ID display. Whalen.

"Who is that?" Dugan asked.

"The only ranch hand I have left," Riley said.

On the off chance that Gandt was at Riley's, Dugan punched Connect and held the phone up to Riley, tilting it so he could hear the conversation.

"Riley?"

"Yeah, what is it?"

"The barn on the south side of the property is on fire!"

"Good God," Riley shouted. "Call the fire department."

The man yelled that he would, and Dugan took the phone, fear riddling him.

He'd wondered where Gandt would take Sage....

What if he'd taken her to Riley's? He could have planned to kill her there, then frame Riley for her murder.

Heart hammering, Dugan jumped in the SUV and tore down the dirt road, slinging gravel and dust in his wake.

"Take me to my place," Riley yelled.

"That's where we're going," Dugan snapped. Although Riley would be going to jail when this was over. "I have a bad feeling Gandt is there with Sage, and that he's behind the fire."

A litany of four-letter words spewed from Riley's mouth. "He was going to set me up."

"Yeah, and probably frame you for it." Dugan couldn't help himself. He enjoyed the terror on Riley's face.

He pressed the pedal to the floor, speeding over the potholes and bumps in the road. The ten miles felt like an eternity, but finally he veered down the drive onto Riley's ranch.

"Turn left up there to go to the south barn," Riley said.

Dugan yanked the steering wheel to the left and careened down the dirt path. Pastureland and trees flew by. He passed a pond and saw flames shooting into the air in the distance.

"Holy hell," Riley said. "If that spreads, my pasture will be ruined."

Dugan didn't give a damn about the man's property.

He phoned the deputy to meet him at Riley's property to arrest the rancher as he zoomed down the narrow road. He wished the fire engine was here, but he'd beat them to it. An old beat-up pickup truck was parked by a shed, and he spotted an elderly man pacing by the fence.

His tires screeched as he slammed on the brakes and

came to a stop. He jumped out and ran toward the burning building.

"Did you see anyone inside?" Dugan shouted.

"I didn't go in," the old man said with a puzzled look on his craggy face. "We didn't have any livestock in there."

But Sage…what about Sage?

The old man hadn't checked because he had no reason to think she'd be inside.

Panic streaked through Dugan. But he didn't hesitate.

"Don't bother to try and get away," he told Riley. He grabbed a blanket from the back of his SUV, wrapped it around himself and ran into the blaze.

Chapter Twenty-One

Sage struggled against the ropes as the fire began to eat the floor and rippled up the walls. The smoke was thick, curling through the air and clogging her lungs.

She was going to die.

And then she'd never know where her son was.

No…she couldn't leave him behind. He needed her.

She kicked the chair over, searching blindly for a sliver of wood to use as a knife. She managed to grab a rough piece that had splintered from one of the rails and clutched it between her fingers. Then she angled and twisted her wrists and hands to get a better stab at the ropes.

Heat seared her body and scalded her back, and she used her feet to push herself away from the burning floor to a clear patch. Her eyes stung from the smoke, and each breath took a mountain of effort. She curled her chin into her chest, breathing out through her mouth and focusing on sawing away at the ropes.

Wood crackled around her, the stall next to her collapsing. Sparks flew as the flames climbed the walls toward the ceiling. The building was so old, places were rotting, and it was going to be engulfed in seconds.

The sliver of wood jabbed her palm, and she winced and dropped it. Panicked, she fumbled to retrieve it and felt heat burn her fingers.

Tears trickled down her cheeks as pain rippled through her, then a piece of the barn loft suddenly crackled and popped, debris flying down to the floor around her.

DUGAN RACED THROUGH the flames to the inside, where the fire blazed in patches across the barn. The raw scent of burning wood and leather swirled in an acrid haze around him. He scrutinized the interior, searching as best he could with the limited visibility.

Tack room to the left, completely engulfed in flames.

Three stalls to the right. Two were ablaze.

Flames inched toward the third.

Smoke clogged the air like a thick gray curtain, forcing him to cover his nose with a handkerchief.

"Sage! Sage, where are you?" Maybe he was wrong, and she wasn't here.

He hoped to hell he *was* wrong.

Wood splintered and crashed from the back. He dodged another patch as he ran toward the last stall. Fire sizzled and licked at the stall door.

"Sage!"

He touched the wooden latch. It was hot. Using the blanket to protect his hand, he pushed it open.

Sage was lying on the floor, her hands and feet tied to a chair. She wasn't moving.

Terror gripped him, and he beat at the flames creeping toward her, slapping out the fire nipping at his boots. His feet were growing hot, but he ripped his knife from his back pocket, sliced through the ropes, then quickly picked Sage up in his arms.

She was so still and limp that fear chased at his calm. But he had to get them out.

"Sage, baby, I've got you." She didn't make a sound, but he thought he detected a breath. Slow and shallow, but she was alive.

He wrapped the blanket around his shoulders, tucked her close to him and covered her with it, then darted from the stall. The front of the barn was sizzling and totally engulfed.

He scanned the interior, searching for a way out. An opening near the back door. Just enough to escape.

He clutched Sage to him, securing her head against his chest and tugging the blanket over her face as he ran through the patches of burning debris and out the back door. Flames crawled up his legs, but he continued running until he was a safe distance away. Then he dropped to the ground, still holding Sage as he beat the flames out with the blanket.

A siren wailed and lights twirled in the night sky as the fire engine raced down the dirt road toward them. They were too late to save the barn.

He hoped to hell they weren't too late to save the woman in his arms.

SAGE STIRRED FROM UNCONSCIOUSNESS, disoriented and choking for a breath.

"Here, miss, you need oxygen." A blurry-looking young woman pushed a mask over her face, and someone squeezed her hand.

"You're okay, Sage. Just relax."

Exhaustion and fatigue claimed her, and she closed her eyes, giving in to it. But her mind refused to shut down. Questions screamed in her head.

What had happened? Where was she? Where was Dugan?

Then reality seeped in, crashing against her, and she jerked and tried to sit up.

"Shh, it's okay, you're safe," Dugan murmured.

She rasped the sheriff's name, then looked through the

haze and saw Dugan looking down at her, his forehead furrowed with worry.

"I called Jaxon. I'll find Gandt, Sage, I promise."

She wanted to believe him, to trust him, but Gandt had gotten away. And…he didn't know where Benji was.

Tears clogged her eyes. If that was true, finding the sheriff didn't matter. She still wouldn't have her son.

She clawed at Dugan's hand, silently begging him to move closer. A strangled sound came from her throat as she tried to say his name.

"Don't try to talk," Dugan whispered. "You need rest."

She shook her head, frantic that he hear her, then shoved at her mask.

The medic tried to adjust it, but she pushed her hand away.

"Dugan…"

Dugan finally realized she needed to tell him something and leaned closer. "What? Do you know where he went?"

She shook her head, her eyes tearing from emotions or smoke, she didn't know which. "Said…Benji…" She broke into a coughing spell.

Dugan clung to her hand. "Did he tell you where Benji is?"

She shook her head again, choking out the words between coughs. "Gandt killed Ron."

"I know, and he sent Lloyd Riley to kill me."

Sage's face paled even more. "Said Benji not with Ron…."

"What?" Dugan sighed deeply. "You're sure?"

She nodded, tears running down her cheeks, like a river.

He wiped them away and pressed a kiss to her lips. "Don't give up. I will find him, Sage, I promise."

Despair threatened to consume her, and she gave in to the fatigue and closed her eyes. She felt Dugan's hand closing around hers, heard his voice whispering to her to hang on, and the paramedics lifted her into the ambulance.

Dugan squeezed her arm. "I'll meet you at the hospital."

She nodded. At least she thought she did. But she was too tired to tell.

Then the ambulance jerked, a siren rent the air and she bounced as the driver raced off toward the hospital and away from the burning barn.

DUGAN HATED THE FEAR in Sage's eyes because it mirrored his own. If he'd been five minutes later, she would have died.

He shut out the thought. She hadn't died, and the medics would take care of her.

He had to find Gandt.

But if Benji wasn't with Lewis, and Gandt didn't know his whereabouts, where was he?

He'd already phoned Jaxon while waiting on the ambulance, and Jaxon agreed to put out a statewide hunt for Gandt.

What the hell should he do now?

Gandt was missing. Lewis dead. Rankins dead. Carol Sue dead.

Who had Benji? Sandra Peyton?

He jumped in his SUV and followed the deputy to the sheriff's office to make sure that he locked Riley up. He half expected Gandt to be cocky enough to be sitting in his office, with his feet propped up.

Did the sheriff know that Sage had survived? That Riley hadn't killed Dugan?

Did he think he'd gotten away?

Itching to know, Dugan decided to check the man's house. If he thought he'd gotten off scot-free, Gandt might be celebrating his good fortune. Or if he was afraid he was about to be caught, he might be packing to run.

Dugan knew where the man lived. Out on the river, by the gorge.

He whipped his SUV in that direction, eager to check it out.

Traffic was nonexistent on the country highway, the wilderness surrounding him as he veered off the main road and drove into the wooded property where Gandt lived.

The driveway was miles long, farm and ranch land sprawling for acres and acres.

Why Gandt was so greedy when he had all this, Dugan would never know.

When he neared the clearing for the house, he slowed and cut his lights.

He rolled up behind a tree and parked, pulled his gun and slipped through the bushes along the edge of the property. The sheriff's car was parked in front of the house, one car door open.

Dugan slowly approached it, bracing for an ambush. But as he crept near the car and looked inside, he saw it was empty.

Breathing out in relief, he ducked low and walked along the fence until he reached the side of the porch, which ran the length of the front of the house.

The door screeched opened, and Gandt appeared. Dugan ducked low and watched, surprised at the sight of Gandt pushing a gray-haired woman in a wheelchair out the door.

"I don't understand why I have to leave," the woman said shrilly.

"Because I'm going away for a few days and can't take care of you, Mother," Gandt said, his tone contrite.

"Can't you hire a nurse like you did before?"

"No, that costs a fortune. Gwen said you can come and stay with her."

The woman laid a hand on Gandt's arm. "But her husband doesn't like me."

"Mother," Gandt said, his patience wearing thin in his voice, "just please try to get along with them. When I straighten things out, I'll come back for you."

He pushed her down a ramp attached to the opposite side of the porch.

"What do you have to get straightened out?" she cried.

Dugan stepped from the shadows, his gun drawn. The woman gasped, and Gandt reached for his weapon.

"Don't," Dugan said. "I'd hate to have to shoot you in front of your mother."

The woman shrieked again. "Please don't hurt us." She clutched Gandt's arm. "Who is this man?"

"My name is Dugan Graystone," Dugan said. "I hate to tell you this, ma'am, but your son is not all you think he is."

Her sharp, angry eyes pierced Dugan like lasers. "You have no right talking to me about my son. What are you, some criminal on the loose?"

"Mother, be quiet," Gandt said through gritted teeth.

"I'm not the criminal here," Dugan said. "Mrs. Gandt, your son tried to have me killed, and he tied Sage Freeport—"

"Shut up," Gandt snarled.

"You don't want your mother to know what kind of man her son really is?"

"My son is a wonderful man. He takes care of this town."

"Mother—"

"He stole land from the ranchers and conned them. Then he shot Ron Lewis." Dugan paused. "Did you kill Wilbur Rankins, too?"

The woman turned shocked, troubled eyes toward Gandt. "Son, tell him that's not so...."

"It is true." Dugan waved his gun toward Gandt. "Now I want to know where Sage Freeport's little boy is."

Gandt walked toward Dugan, his eyes oozing steam as if he refused to admit to any wrongdoing. "You have a lot of nerve coming to my house, carrying a gun and making accusations." He handed his mother his phone. "Call my deputy and tell him to get over here right now."

Dugan stepped forward, unrelenting. Did Gandt really think he could get away with all this? "Fine, tell him to come, Mrs. Gandt. Also tell him he'll be arresting your son for murder."

The older woman gasped and clutched at her chest.

Dugan dug the gun barrel into Gandt's belly. "Now, where is Benji Freeport?"

Chapter Twenty-Two

A siren wailed, headlights lighting a path on the house as Jaxon roared up in his Texas Ranger truck.

Gandt cursed. "Let me take my mother back inside," he said to Dugan. "Then we'll talk."

Dugan felt sorry for the older woman, but he shook his head. No way did he intend to let Gandt out of his sight. Not even for a minute.

Mrs. Gandt curled her arthritic hands in her lap, around the phone, fear mingling with doubt in her expression now. Had she suspected her son was helping to swindle the town? Or that he was capable of murder?

Jaxon's car door slammed, and he strode toward them.

"Sheriff Gandt," Jaxon said. "You are under arrest for the murder of Ron Lewis and for the attempted murder of Sage Freeport." He read the sheriff his rights.

Gandt reared his head, shock on his face. He hadn't known Sage had survived. "You have no evidence of any crime I've committed. I'm the law around here."

"As a matter of fact, Sage Freeport is alive and she will testify that you tied her into the barn and set fire to it."

Gandt's mother gasped, her expression reeking of shock. "No, no…tell them, son, you didn't do those awful things."

"Lloyd Riley also claims that you blackmailed him into helping and ordered him to kill me," Dugan added.

"And speaking of evidence," Jaxon said, "I just got confirmation from ballistics that the bullet that killed Wilbur Rankins is the same caliber you use, so add on another murder charge." Jaxon took handcuffs from inside his jacket. "Put your hands behind you, Gandt."

Gandt shifted to the balls of his feet, jerking his hands as Jaxon grabbed his arms. "Mother, call Sherman, my lawyer," he snarled.

"No one is going to get you off," Dugan said. "Because you're going to pay for what you've done to Sage and to the people in this town."

Jaxon snapped the handcuffs around Gandt's wrists, then spun him back around. "Do you know what happened to Benji Freeport? Did you kill him, too?"

Gandt shook his head. "I told that woman he wasn't with Lewis. I have no idea where he is."

Dugan ground his molars. Gandt was already facing murder and attempted murder charges, along with fraud charges.

Why wouldn't he tell them where the boy was?

Because he really didn't know. Which meant they might never find Benji.

SAGE WOKE IN the hospital to find Dugan sitting by her bed. He looked worn out, his face thick with beard stubble, his eyes blurry from lack of sleep, his expression grim.

She broke into another coughing spell, and Dugan handed her a glass of water and held the straw for her to drink. "What time is it?"

"About four in the morning. You okay?"

Was she? She'd nearly died. And she still didn't have her son back. "I'll live," she said softly.

A pained smile twisted at his lips. "I got Gandt. He's in jail."

Sage sighed and took another sip of water.

"He blackmailed Lloyd Riley into helping him and ordered him to kill me."

Sage's eyes flared with shock. "Did he tell you where Benji is?"

A darkness fell over Dugan's face, making her stomach tighten with nerves. "Dugan?"

"He claims he has no idea, that Benji wasn't with Lewis when he killed him."

Sage closed her eyes, hating the despair overwhelming her. She'd thought for certain that finding Ron's killer would lead them to her son.

"I won't give up," Dugan said in a gruff voice.

"But Carol Sue, the woman we thought might have Benji, is dead."

"True, but Sandra Peyton is still unaccounted for."

"I know. Thanks, Dugan." Her earlier ordeal weighed her down. Or maybe it was defeat.

Sage closed her eyes, willing sleep to take her away from the memory of Gandt leaving her in that burning barn.

And the reality that she still had to face another Christmas without her little boy.

DUGAN SETTLED ONTO the recliner beside Sage and watched her sleep. Although the danger was over for her, he couldn't bear to leave her alone tonight.

Not with knowing he'd failed to find Benji.

And not with images of her lying in that blazing fire, nearly dead, tormenting him. He could have lost her tonight.

Lost her? He'd never had her....

The realization that he cared so damn much that it hurt made him stand and pace to the window. Cobra Creek was quiet tonight.

The deputy would temporarily take over for Sheriff

Gandt. Once the red tape was handled, the ranchers who'd been duped would get their land back.

But Sage was right back where she was when he'd decided to help her.

Making matters worse, Christmas was almost here. The image of that pitiful little Christmas tree with the unopened package under it taunted him.

Sage should have a full-size tree with dozens of gifts beneath it, and her little boy should be home making cookies with her and opening presents Christmas morning.

He considered buying her a gift, but nothing he could buy would make up for the void in her life that losing Benji had left.

She stirred, restless, and made a mewling sound in her throat, then thrashed at the covers. He soothed her with soft words, gently stroking her hair with one hand, until she calmed.

More than anything, he wanted to bring Benji back to her.

He'd never felt this emotional attachment before. This intense drive to please someone.

God...he was falling for her. Maybe he had been from the moment she'd looked up at him with those trusting, green eyes.

But what was he going to do about it?

He couldn't tell her or pressure her. Sage had already suffered too much. And she was vulnerable.

Besides, why would she want him when he'd failed her?

He finally fell asleep in the chair but woke a couple of hours later when the nurse returned to take Sage's vitals. He stepped out for coffee and to grab some breakfast while they helped her dress.

By the time he returned, the doctor was dismissing her.

"I'll drive you home, Sage."

She thanked him but remained silent as the nurse

wheeled her to the exit and on the drive home. When they arrived at the inn, the Christmas lights mocked him.

"Thank you, Dugan. I have to go shower and get out of these clothes. They stink like smoke."

She was right. Worse, they were probably a reminder of her near-death experience. He climbed out and walked her to the door.

"I can stay with you for a while if you want."

Sage shook her head, fumbling with the key as she tried to unlock the door. "I need to be alone."

Dugan took the keys from her and unlocked the door, not ready to leave her. He needed to hold her, to know that she was still alive and safe. That there might be hope for the two of them.

But she stepped inside and blocked the doorway. "Good night, Dugan."

Dugan reached up to take her hand, but she pulled it away and clenched the door edge.

"I'm not giving up, I will find Benji," Dugan said earnestly. Sandra Peyton might be the key.

She gave a small nod of acceptance, yet the light he'd seen in her eyes had faded. Damn, she'd lost hope.

The hope that had helped her survive the past two years.

She closed the door in his face, and Dugan cursed.

Maybe she didn't return the feelings he'd developed for her. But he'd be damned if he'd let her give up on her son.

Sage waited until Dugan left, then walked to the kitchen for a glass of water. The Christmas tree with Benji's present sat on the table, looking as bare and lonely as she felt.

Dugan said he wasn't giving up.

But she was smart enough to realize that they'd reached a dead end. If Gandt didn't know where Benji was, who did?

Sandra Peyton.

The woman could be anywhere by now. If she'd taken Benji knowing Ron abducted him, she had probably gone into hiding.

Angry and frustrated and full of despair, she took the water to her bedroom and jumped in the shower. The hot spray felt heavenly as it washed away the stench of the smoke.

But the memory of Gandt coldly leaving her to die couldn't be erased so easily.

The silence in the house echoed around her, eerie and lonely, as she dried off, pulled on a pair of pajamas and collapsed onto her bed.

Dugan's scent lingered, teasing her senses and making her body ache for his comforting arms and touch.

But she couldn't allow herself to need him. She had to stand on her own.

The only thing she wanted right now was the little boy who'd stolen her heart the day he was born.

She had nothing to give to a man like Dugan. A man who deserved so much more than a broken woman like her.

Chapter Twenty-Three

Christmas Eve

Dugan had called Sage several times the past two days, but she had cut him off. Not that she hadn't been polite. She'd made it clear that if he learned anything new about her son, he should call her.

But she obviously didn't want a personal relationship with him.

Because he'd let her down. He'd promised to bring her son home and he hadn't, and she would never forgive him.

He let Hiram and his other two hands go early so they could spend Christmas Eve with their families.

Dugan would spend another one alone.

Normally the holidays meant nothing. Being alone didn't bother him. He loved his land and his work and his freedom.

He didn't know how to be part of a family.

So why did his chest have a sharp pain to it because he wasn't spending the night with Sage? Why couldn't he stop thinking about her, wondering what she was doing, if she was baking for Christmas dinner, if the inn smelled like cinnamon, if she was lighting a candle for her son, in hopes that it would bring him back to her?

Dammit.

He rode back to the stables, dismounted and brushed down his favorite horse, then stowed him in his stall. Just as he walked across the pasture toward his house, his cell phone buzzed.

Hoping it was Sage, he snatched it up, but Jaxon's voice echoed back.

"Dugan here."

"That reporter, Ashlynn Fontaine, called. Said she got another tip from that tip line."

Dugan's pulse jackknifed. "Tell me about it."

"This woman claims she thinks she's seen Benji, that she works with this waitress named Sandy Lewis, who has a little boy named Jordan. When she saw the news report, she realized Jordan was the spittin' image of Benji."

Sandy Lewis—Sandra Peyton Lewis? "What's the address?"

"I'm texting it to you now."

Dugan ended the call and referred to the text. He had to check this lead out. But the last time he'd taken Sage with him, it had been nearly devastating for her.

This time he'd go alone.

If Jordan turned out to be Benji and he recovered the little boy, he'd surprise her. If not, she would never know.

SAGE FORCED HERSELF out of bed each day, but the depression that seized her was nearly as paralyzing as it was the first few weeks after Benji disappeared.

She had to face the fact that she might never see her son again.

Could she bear to go on without him?

The women's group at church surprised her by stopping by with baked goods Christmas Eve morning. She had joined the group two months after Benji disappeared because she'd woken up one day with no desire to live.

It had scared her to think that she might do something

crazy like take her own life. Worse, if she did and Benji was found, she wouldn't be around to take care of him.

That day had driven her to ask for help, and she'd gone to the church seeking solace and prayer. She had found it, both with the pastor and the women who'd embraced her and revitalized her spirit with their positive thinking and compassion.

Today she felt as if she'd regressed. They must have sensed it, because the coffee and goodies were simply a backdrop to let her talk.

She hugged them all goodbye and thanked them for coming, then waved as they hurried to their cars. Five women with five different backgrounds and lives. Families of all sorts. Troubles of their own.

But they had come to her when she needed emotional support the most.

Wiping at tears, she cleaned up the kitchen and stored the tins of cookies on the kitchen bar, setting them out as she would for Benji. The Christmas plate with reindeer on it awaited the cookies and milk they would have left for Santa.

The women had reminded her of the candlelight service at six, and she had promised she would attend. Determined to keep herself from spiraling downward, she spent the afternoon wrapping the presents she'd bought for the children's hospital and the women's shelter, then stacked them all in her car to carry to the church.

A group would disperse them in the morning to make sure that children in need had Christmas, like all the other kids in the world.

She had volunteered last year. Maybe she'd go this year, as well.

Anything to help her get through the long, lonely day.

Her mind turned to Dugan and the numerous calls he'd

made. She wanted to see him, missed him in a way she'd never expected to.

And not just because he'd been helping her.

Because he'd stood by, solid and strong. He was handsome, sexy, protective, honorable. He owned and worked his own ranch, but he also worked search-and-rescue missions for strangers.

All qualities Ron and Trace had never possessed.

But Dugan deserved someone who could love and take care of him, not an empty shell of a woman who had to force herself to get out of bed to face the day.

DUGAN FOUND SANDY'S HOUSE fifty miles from Cobra Creek. It was a nondescript wooden house with a fenced yard, a swing set in the back and a gray minivan in the drive.

At first glance, it appeared to be homey. Christmas lights twinkled from the awnings, a handmade wreath garnished the front door and a tree complete with trimmings was visible through a picture window. A bike with training wheels sat in the front yard, and a soccer ball had been left in the driveway.

Was this woman simply a mother or a kidnapper?

He was just about to climb out when the front door opened, and a woman stepped outside, pulling a rolling suitcase. She wore sunglasses and a scarf and seemed to be in a hurry. She glanced up and down the street, opened the back of the minivan and tossed her suitcase inside, then shut the door.

She rushed back to the house and seconds later, emerged with a little boy in tow, a jungle backpack slung over his shoulder. Dugan sat up straighter to get a better look. The kid was the right size, but he was wearing a baseball cap, and Dugan couldn't see his face.

She tugged the boy's hand, but he drew back, and she

stooped down and appeared to be reprimanding him. The boy dropped his head, allowing her to lead him to the van.

Dugan almost interceded then. It looked as though Sandy was getting ready to take a trip. Had Gandt's arrest spooked her enough to run?

Deciding she might be meeting up with an accomplice, he waited until she backed from the drive, then followed her. He kept his distance, and maintained a steady speed so as not to alarm her.

A half hour later, she turned into the bus station. Dugan parked a couple of spaces from her and watched to see if she was meeting someone. She climbed out, looking over her shoulder and all around the parking lot as if she feared someone was after her.

Seemingly satisfied, she retrieved her suitcase, then pushed open the boy's door and helped him from the van. After kneeling to speak to him, she took his hand and ushered him toward the bus station.

Dugan didn't intend to let her get away.

He strode toward the entrance and caught up with her just as she stepped up to the ticket counter. The boy kept his head down, and she had a death grip on his hand.

"I need one adult and one child's ticket to New Mexico." She fished out ID and a wad of cash.

"You're not going anywhere, Miss Peyton," Dugan said in a low voice near her ear. "Not until you answer some questions."

She gasped and turned around, wide-eyed. "Who are you?"

"A friend of Sage Freeport."

Her face paled, and she tried to tug her arm from his grip, but he held her firmly. "Now, unless you want me to pull my gun and make a scene here, do as I say."

She stilled, and he saw her glance at the boy in panic.

The little guy made a frightened sound, which ripped at Dugan's heart.

"It's okay, son. I'm not here to hurt you." He hated to scare him, but if the child was Sage's son, he was saving the boy. He nudged the woman. "Walk back outside to your van."

She darted furtive looks around her as if she was debating whether or not to scream for help, but he opened his jacket enough to reveal his gun, and she sucked in a breath and headed toward the van. When they reached it, he ordered her up against the door.

"Please don't hurt my son," she cried.

"I'm not here to hurt him," Dugan said, intentionally lowering his voice to calm the kid, who looked as if he might bolt any second.

"Then what do you want? I have some cash—"

"This is not a robbery." Dugan gestured toward the boy, who had huddled up against her with his head buried in her stomach. "I'm here because of Benji."

Her eyes flared with panic, and the boy suddenly whipped his head around.

Dugan stooped down to his eye level and reached for the boy's hat. "Are you Benji Freeport?"

"His name is Jordan," the woman cried. "He's my son."

The hat slid off to reveal a head of choppy, blondish hair and eyes that looked familiar.

Sage's deep green eyes.

Remembering Sage said he had an extra piece of cartilage in his ear, he lifted the boy's hat. Yes. Just like the picture.

"You are Benji, aren't you, son?"

The boy fidgeted but didn't respond.

Dugan removed a photo that Sage had given him of the two of them from his pocket and showed it to him. "This woman, Sage, she's my friend. She wanted me to find you.

She's your real mother, and she's been looking for you ever since you disappeared two years ago."

The boy's face crumpled. "Mama?"

"Yes," Dugan said softly. "Your mama loves you, and she misses you and wants you to come home."

Benji angled his head toward Sandra Peyton, his look sharp with accusations. "You said she didn't want me anymore."

Dugan's pulse hammered.

"She didn't, but I wanted you." Sandra's chin quivered, and she began to cry. "I love you, Jordan. I'm your mama now."

The boy looked confused, his gaze turning back to Dugan. "Sage is your mother," Dugan said. "And she never gave you up, never told this woman she could have you." He kept his voice gentle. "She loves you so much. She's kept your Christmas tree up with your presents under it, just waiting on you to come back and open them."

Benji's little face contorted with anguish.

"Do you remember what happened, Benji? A man named Ron Lewis took you one morning...."

Tears pooled in his eyes, but Benji nodded as if the memory was slowly returning.

A strangled sound came from Benji's throat. "He took me to the river and told me to go with her."

Dugan glared at Sandra. "You and Lewis were a couple. You planned the kidnapping together."

Sandra broke down in tears. "I loved Ron and he loved me. We hadn't seen each other since I had that miscarriage. But he called me one day and said he was about to make a big windfall, and that he wanted us to be a family." Her voice broke. "But I couldn't get pregnant again."

Disgust churned inside Dugan. "So Lewis cozied up to Sage so he could get to know Benji?"

She wiped at tears. "He didn't want Benji to be afraid when he left with him, so he got to know him. And it would have worked, too. We would have all been together if someone hadn't killed Ron."

Dugan punched Jaxon's number. "I have Sandra Peyton and Benji Freeport at the bus station. I need backup."

As soon as Jaxon arrested Sandra, he'd take Benji home to Sage, where he belonged.

SAGE LET HERSELF into the inn, grateful for her friends who'd convinced her to attend the service. Of course, when they'd lit candles, turned off the church lights and sung "Silent Night" in the candlelight, she remembered the joy on Benji's face as he'd held his candle up, and she nearly collapsed in tears.

The Christmas lights twinkled as she flipped on the light switch, and the scent of cinnamon and apples swirled toward her from her earlier baking.

Maybe she'd take the baked goods to the seniors' center in the morning. She couldn't stand the thought of eating cinnamon rolls by herself. She twisted the locket, her heart thumping. She thought she'd gotten accustomed to being alone, but tonight she ached for Benji.

Dugan's face flashed in her mind, and she wondered where he was tonight. He hadn't mentioned any family.

Was he still looking for Benji, or had he given up?

She dropped her keys in the ceramic pot on the table by the door, then decided to light the candles in the kitchen and living room.

She had just poured herself a glass of wine and started to play her collection of Christmas music when a knock sounded at the door. Probably someone else from church, checking on her.

She hurried to the front door, prepared to assure her visitor that she was fine, but Dugan stood on the other side.

He looked so utterly handsome that her knees nearly buckled.

"Sage, I had to see you."

The urgency in his tone sent a streak of panic through her. "Is something wrong?"

"No." A small smile tugged at his mouth, and his eyes were sparkling, making him look even more handsome. Come to think of it, she'd never seen him smile. "I have a present for you," he said gruffly.

Sage twisted the locket again. "You didn't need to get me anything."

"Yes, I did. I made you a promise, and I keep my promises." Then he stepped to the side, and Sage's heart went wild as she saw the little boy beside him.

Emotions choked her. After two years, she'd been afraid she wouldn't recognize her son when she saw him again, but she instantly knew him.

Dugan had kept his promise. He had found Benji.

She dropped to her knees, soaking in the sight of him, desperate to pull him into her arms. But he looked hesitant, frightened, wary.

"Benji?"

She glanced up at Dugan, needing answers.

"Lewis took him to Sandra Peyton. He's been living with her for the past two years."

Sage wiped at the tears streaming down her face.

"She told him that you gave him up," Dugan said almost apologetically, "that you didn't want him anymore."

"Oh, God..." Pain rocked through Sage. Her poor little boy thought she'd abandoned him.

She took Benji's hands in hers and gave him a smile. She had to convince him she'd always loved him. "Benji, I never gave you up. I would never do that." She brushed at a tear. "One morning I got up, and Ron had taken you without telling me. I called the police, I called the news station, we put the story on TV, I did everything I could to find you."

He had grown taller and lost some of his chubby baby fat, but his eyes were just as bright and sweet. "I love you so much, Benji. I prayed every day that I'd find you."

He lifted his chin, big tears in his eyes. "Mommy?"

"Yes, sweet boy. I'm your mommy." She nearly sobbed at the feel of his tiny palm in hers. "Come on, I want to show you something."

She led him into the kitchen and showed him the table-top tree, leaving Dugan in the foyer. "Remember when you used to decorate this for your room? It was your own tree."

His eyes widened as he stared at it. Then she pointed out the presents with his name on them. "This one in Santa paper was the gift I bought for you the year you disappeared. Do you remember it? You were only three, but you shook it every day and tried to guess what was in it."

He wrinkled his forehead as if he was trying to recall the memory.

"I bought this one in the snowman paper for you last year," she said as she gestured toward another package. "And this one wrapped in reindeer paper this year, because I was hoping I'd find you and you'd come home."

He looked torn as if he wanted to believe her but was still on the verge. She hated Sandra Peyton for what she'd done to him, for lying to him.

Then she had an idea. "Let me show you your room. I kept it just the way it was."

She led him up the stairs and to his bedroom, the room she hadn't changed since he left. Inside, she walked over to the bed and picked up the special blanket he'd slept with and held it out to him. "See, I saved your blankie. I knew one day that you'd come home."

His little chin wobbled as tears filled his eyes. "Mommy?"

"Yes, baby, I've missed you so much." She opened her arms, and he fell into them, his tears mingling with hers as they savored the reunion.

Chapter Twenty-Four

By the time, Sage and Benji came back downstairs, Dugan was gone. A pang of disappointment tugged at her. He obviously felt as if he'd done his job and had gone home.

But she missed him, anyway.

Still, her son was finally home. It was the day she'd been waiting for. And soothing Benji's fears and rebuilding his trust were the only things that mattered tonight.

They spent the evening making sugar cookies and talking about the past. At times they were both sad, but she tried to help him focus on the fact that they were together again, and he was safe.

Much to her relief, Benji indicated that Sandra had been good to him, had been patient and played with him and read him stories.

Of course, they'd moved around a lot. Sandra had probably known that one day the truth would catch up with her.

Sage fought against the bitterness eating at her. She was grateful Sandra had loved Benji, but the woman had stolen all that time and precious memories from her.

And Benji had suffered the trauma.

But focusing on the past they'd lost would only keep her from enjoying the future, so she vowed to let go of the bitterness.

She read him Christmas stories and tucked him in, then watched him fall asleep, soaking in his features.

When she crawled in bed that night, she was happier than she'd been in ages. She and Benji were a family again.

But there was one thing missing.

Dugan.

She sat up, her heart stuttering. Oh, goodness.

While she'd been guarding her heart and looking for her son, she'd fallen in love with Dugan.

What was she going to do about it?

Did Dugan have feelings for her?

Dugan missed Sage like crazy. But she needed time to reunite with her son. Not pressure from him.

But when he rose Christmas morning and combed his ranch house, the deafening silence got to him. He couldn't help imagining Benji running down to find Santa's presents and Sage making breakfast for the two of them.

Work and the land had always been his first loves.

But his life felt empty now.

He suddenly felt antsy and had to get out. A ride across his ranch would do him good, help him clear his head, pass some time and take his mind off the woman who'd stolen a piece of his soul the past few days. And her kid, who'd won his heart the minute he laid eyes on him.

He combed the property, examining fences in case they needed mending, then checking livestock. Hiram and his other two hands had done a good job taking care of things while he worked the case. Now it was time for him to get back to it.

By the time he reached the farmhouse, his stomach was growling. He had nothing in the house to cook, certainly no holiday dinner.

Maybe he'd drive into town for a burger. That is, if the diner was open. Most folks were home with family today.

He guided his horse up to the house, slowing when he saw Sage's car. What was she doing here?

His heart began to race. He steered the horse to the rail and dismounted, then saw Sage and Benji sitting in the porch swing. Sage had her arm slung around Benji, and he was leaning into her as they rocked the swing back and forth.

It was the most beautiful sight he'd ever seen.

His heart took a funny leap, his mind roaring down a dangerous path. What would it be like to have a family to come home to?

To have Benji and Sage in his life forever?

Sage looked up at him with a tentative smile, but Benji vaulted up and leaned over the porch rail. "Your horse is cool, Mr. Dugan."

Gone was the traumatized kid from the night before. One night at home with his mother had the boy smiling and at ease.

"Thanks. If your mama agrees, I'll take you riding sometime."

Sage stood, walked to the rail and leaned over it, then looked down at him. "Maybe you can take us both out?"

The subtle question in her eyes made him smile. Was she flirting with him?

"Maybe I will," he said with a wink.

She laughed softly in response, and he realized she *was* flirting.

One night with her son had erased the shadows and pain from her eyes.

Benji ran down the steps. "Can I pet him?"

"Sure." Dugan showed him how to gently rub the horse's mane.

"We brought dinner for you," Sage said. "That is, if you don't have plans."

Dugan met her gaze. "That was real nice of you."

She walked down the steps and rubbed a finger along his arm. "It wasn't nice. I missed you, Dugan."

He liked this side of her. He angled his head, heat sizzling between them. And something more. An attraction that went far beneath the surface. He admired her. Liked her.

Loved her.

"I missed you, too," he said in a gruff voice.

For a brief moment, his breath stalled as he waited on her to make the next move.

Finally she lifted a finger to his lips. "Did you?"

A grin split his face. She was fishing for a compliment? "Yes." He suddenly couldn't help himself. That big rambling farmhouse needed her and Benji in it.

He yanked her up against him. "I'm in love with you, Sage."

Her eyes sparkled as she looped her arms around his neck. "Good, 'cause I'm in love with you, too."

Then she rose on her tiptoes, closed her lips over his and kissed him. Dugan had never felt anything so sweet, so wonderful.

And suddenly he knew what being in a family was like. He would make one with Sage and Benji, and he would never let them go.

* * * * *

Look for award-winning author Rita Herron's next book, COLD CASE IN CHEROKEE CROSSING, on sale in December 2014. You'll find it wherever Harlequin Intrigue books are sold!

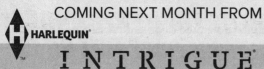

COMING NEXT MONTH FROM

HARLEQUIN®

INTRIGUE®

Available November 18, 2014

#1533 DELIVERANCE AT CARDWELL RANCH
Cardwell Cousins • by B.J. Daniels
When Deputy Sheriff Austin Cardwell rescues a woman with no memory in a blizzard, it's only the beginning. Austin vows to uncover her true identity...before her violent past destroys any hope of a future together.

#1534 KIDNAPPING IN KENDALL COUNTY
Sweetwater Ranch • by Delores Fossen
After her investigation into her daughter's kidnapping blows FBI Agent Austin Duran's cover, rancher's daughter Rosalie McKinnon must team up with the rogue cowboy—the very man who once cost Rosalie everything.

#1535 COLD CASE IN CHEROKEE CROSSING
by Rita Herron
Desperate to save her brother from death row, Avery Tierney turns to Texas Ranger Jaxon Ward for help to clear him—but investigating Avery's tragic past will put both their lives and hearts in danger....

#1536 CHRISTMAS JUSTICE
by Robin Perini
Can on-the-run CIA analyst Laurel McCallister and mysterious Sheriff Garrett Galloway uncover the identity of a traitor before the past catches up with them?

#1537 WITNESS PROTECTION
The Campbells of Creek Bend • by Barb Han
First rule of Witness Protection—*never* get involved with the person under protection. But when U.S. Marshal Nick Campbell grows too close to witness Sadie Brooks, how far will he go to save the woman he can't stop thinking about?

#1538 EAGLE'S LAST STAND
Copper Canyon • by Aimée Thurlo
Scarred by life, and from a recent deadly assault, undercover FBI agent Rick Cloud returns home only to find his father murdered and his family under attack. Catching the killer might just cost him Kim Nelson, the one woman who can heal his damaged heart....

YOU CAN FIND MORE INFORMATION ON UPCOMING HARLEQUIN® TITLES, FREE EXCERPTS AND MORE AT WWW.HARLEQUIN.COM.

HICNM1114

REQUEST YOUR FREE BOOKS!
2 FREE NOVELS PLUS 2 FREE GIFTS!

♦HARLEQUIN®

INTRIGUE®

BREATHTAKING ROMANTIC SUSPENSE

YES! Please send me 2 FREE Harlequin Intrigue® novels and my 2 FREE gifts (gifts are worth about $10). After receiving them, if I don't wish to receive any more books, I can return the shipping statement marked "cancel." If I don't cancel, I will receive 6 brand-new novels every month and be billed just $4.74 per book in the U.S. or $5.24 per book in Canada. That's a savings of at least 14% off the cover price! It's quite a bargain! Shipping and handling is just 50¢ per book in the U.S. and 75¢ per book in Canada.* I understand that accepting the 2 free books and gifts places me under no obligation to buy anything. I can always return a shipment and cancel at any time. Even if I never buy another book, the two free books and gifts are mine to keep forever.

182/382 HDN F42N

Name _____ (PLEASE PRINT) _____

Address _____ Apt. # _____

City _____ State/Prov. _____ Zip/Postal Code _____

Signature (if under 18, a parent or guardian must sign) _____

Mail to the **Harlequin® Reader Service:**
IN U.S.A.: P.O. Box 1867, Buffalo, NY 14240-1867
IN CANADA: P.O. Box 609, Fort Erie, Ontario L2A 5X3
Are you a subscriber to Harlequin Intrigue books
and want to receive the larger-print edition?
Call 1-800-873-8635 or visit www.ReaderService.com.

* Terms and prices subject to change without notice. Prices do not include applicable taxes. Sales tax applicable in N.Y. Canadian residents will be charged applicable taxes. Offer not valid in Quebec. This offer is limited to one order per household. Not valid for current subscribers to Harlequin Intrigue books. All orders subject to credit approval. Credit or debit balances in a customer's account(s) may be offset by any other outstanding balance owed by or to the customer. Please allow 4 to 6 weeks for delivery. Offer available while quantities last.

Your Privacy—The Harlequin® Reader Service is committed to protecting your privacy. Our Privacy Policy is available online at www.ReaderService.com or upon request from the Harlequin Reader Service.

We make a portion of our mailing list available to reputable third parties that offer products we believe may interest you. If you prefer that we not exchange your name with third parties, or if you wish to clarify or modify your communication preferences, please visit us at www.ReaderService.com/consumerchoice or write to us at Harlequin Reader Service Preference Service, P.O. Box 9062, Buffalo, NY 14269. Include your complete name and address.

HI13R

"Maybe you don't understand the fine line between snooping and jail. Breaking and entering is—"

"I'm going with you." Donning a hat and gloves, Gillian turned to look at him.

Austin was smiling at her as if amused.

"What?" she said, suddenly feeling uncomfortable under his scrutiny. She knew it was silly. He'd seen her at her absolute worst.

"You just look so…cute," he said. "Clearly, breaking the law excites you."

She smiled in spite of herself. It had been a while since a man had complimented her. But it wasn't breaking the law that excited her.

She breathed in the freezing air. It stung her lungs, but made her feel more alive than she had in years. Fear drove her steps along with hope.

At the dark alley, Austin slowed. It was late enough that there were lights on in the houses.

"Come on," Austin said, and they started to turn down the alley.

A vehicle came around the corner, moving slowly. Gillian felt the headlights wash over them, and she let out a worried sound as she froze in midstep.

Her moment of panic didn't subside when she saw that it was a sheriff's department vehicle.

"Austin?" she whispered, not sure what to do.

He turned to her and pulled her into his arms. Her mouth opened in surprise, and the next thing she knew, he was kissing her. At first, she was too stunned to react. But after a moment, she put her arms around his neck and lost herself in the kiss.

As the headlights of the sheriff's car washed over them, she let out a small helpless moan as Austin deepened the kiss, drawing her even closer.

The sheriff's car went on past, and she felt a pang of regret. Slowly, Austin drew back a little. His gaze locked with hers, and for a moment they stood like that, their quickened warm breaths coming out in white clouds.

"Sorry."

She shook her head. She wasn't sorry. She felt…light-headed, happy, as if helium-filled. She thought she might drift off into the night if he let go of her.

"Are you okay?" he asked, looking worried.

She touched the tip of her tongue to her lower lip. "Great. Never better."

Find out what happens next in
DELIVERANCE AT CARDWELL RANCH
by New York Times bestselling author B.J. Daniels,
available December 2014,
only from Harlequin Intrigue.

"Did you come here to kill me?" he demanded, still
whispering.

"If necessary."

Except a dead man couldn't tell her what she needed
to know. But she would have pulled the trigger if it'd
come down to it. Unfortunately, she no longer had a gun
as a bargaining tool. She only had shaky hands. Shaky
body, too, and her heart just kept pounding.

The moments crawled by. He was still staring at her
and obviously waiting for an explanation. The only
sounds were their rough breaths and the rain pinging
against the window.

"Pretend," he finally snapped.

Rosalie didn't get a chance to ask what the heck that
meant before his mouth went to her neck. He nuzzled it,
as if kissing her, but he was still mumbling profanity, and

his jaw muscles were way too tight for this to be a real kissing session.

So, what was this? Some kind of act for the person on the other end of the camera? If so, why was he trying to cover for her?

"I'm not leaving without answers," Rosalie whispered. "And I want these babies safely out of here and back where they belong."

"Pretend we're having sex or you might not be leaving at all. You'll be dead. And so will I."

That was the only warning she got before the pretense went into full swing.

He fumbled between them, pretending to unzip his jeans.

"If necessary?" he said, repeating her response to his question of *Did you come here to kill me?* "If you're not here for revenge, they why did you come?"

"I'm looking for my baby," she said. Her mouth trembled. And she felt her heart breaking all over again.

To find out what happens next, look for USA TODAY *bestselling author Delores Fossen's* **KIDNAPPING IN KENDALL COUNTY,** *part of her* **SWEETWATER RANCH** *series. Available December 2014 wherever Harlequin® Intrigue® books and ebooks are sold!*